D1339573

THE MEMOIRS OF
A VENUS LACKEY

by the same author

DANDY IN ASPIC

DEREK MARLOWE

THE MEMOIRS OF
A VENUS LACKEY

JONATHAN CAPE
THIRTY BEDFORD SQUARE
LONDON

FIRST PUBLISHED 1968
© 1968 BY DEREK MARLOWE

JONATHAN CAPE LTD, 30 BEDFORD SQUARE, WC1

SBN   224 61308 1

PRINTED IN GREAT BRITAIN BY
EBENEZER BAYLIS AND SON LTD
THE TRINITY PRESS, WORCESTER, AND LONDON
ON PAPER MADE BY JOHN DICKINSON AND CO. LTD
BOUND BY A. W. BAIN AND CO. LTD, LONDON

CONTENTS

TO SUKIE
WITH LOVE

We have not sighed deep, laughed free,
   Starved, feasted, despaired—been happy.

And nobody calls you a dunce,
   And people suppose me clever:
This could but have happened once,
   And we missed it, we lost it for ever.

                    Robert Browning

FOREWORD

If I had any sense, I would pack this whole damn thing up now and be done with it. There is no earthly reason why I should allow myself to be crucified by yet another re-run of my sordid, pathetic and (dare I say it? Yes, I dare) lecherous life, merely to kill time while He makes up His mind. Enough's enough—hasn't every newspaper from here to Viña del Mar (wherever that is) had a field day on my account for the past fifteen years? And haven't I made it clear a million times that the matinée idol of yesteryear has now turned crepuscular, even nocturnal if need be, and that all I desire now is a pure, cleansed and celibate soul? How often I (*a naked breast cruelly sassies across my mental vision, devil sent. Soft it must be to the touch, cool, delicate to the back of the wrist. Why only one?*) recall my pedigree of past lovers with a shaking of the head, and a devout genuflection to sobriety, reaching such a state of absolution that I expect a canonization in the post any day now. If there was a post in here, which there isn't. As I wait for Him. To make up His mind.

New paragraph. You see how I tread water like a dog or Christ as I struggle to begin (and we're already on page nine, and God knows what number that is sire to). But begin I must, if He is to cast my lot the right way, and you are to get on with the business of life, which is not in this book or the next, or in any other and never will be. This is about *my* life, and even that can only be curiosity now, for I am dead and in my coffin and done with it all. And that, *that*, may clarify my state of mind to you—Catesby will be my witness, dear, dear, dam-ned Catesby — and yet, heaven help me, I've tried. Oh, how I've tried.

Perhaps my failure is partly due to the fact that I could never, deep down, accept the simple truth that I was brought into the world from a female womb. Never could I honestly accept that, despite the few shreds of evidence contrary to my belief. For to me, you see, I feel I never ever left it, and that all the subsequent post-embryonic experiences were merely some kind of Divine gesture fed into my walnut brain at conception, like a printed circuit, in order to placate my dormant foetus. Something to pass the time. Which just goes to show what a rare fellow you are dealing with, and if it was a toss-up between this and *War and Peace*, you've made a wise choice. Not only will you find me undeniably more fascinating, but I am also thinner. And if you laughed at that last sentence, funnier as well, I suppose.

Oh God, why did I have to believe in you? If only, instead of all this suspense, I could just be silent upon a peak in Darien. Three and a half days in my coffin and still nothing. Nothing. Is it because I decided to take my life in my own hands that you tease me so? But you urge us to practise self-denial, and what is suicide if not the ultimate demonstration of self-denial?

I'm not asking for Archangel Gabriel, just anything to relieve me from this cliff-hanger. Worse, I've just discovered that my zip-fly is undone, and the fools, the fools (*Dahlia, Palsy, Catesby and Co.*), have embalmed me with my arms crossed.

*   *   *

Ten days and still in my own limbo. Perhaps the Roll-Call is in reverse alphabetical order, and He's not going to get to the Cs for a month or more. At least, that's how I'm treating the whole affair. I've nowhere else to go otherwise, so there's no use getting paranoic about it. He's probably very busy, and I'm not surprised, what with all the attractive brochures He's been circulating since the year dot. And even that's a fallacy, for according to Suetonius (of all people) Jesus Christ, His Son, was born in 4 B.C., which strikes me, to say the least, as rather bad timing. So, all in all, I'm not surprised I've been miscalculated for the present.

So let me begin. As you are well aware, being men of the world, I have been branded as a lecher, a fornicator, a creature dedicated to making nothing else but love. *Love!* How regrettably far from the truth that word is in my case. How bitterly far from the truth. For how can *I* talk of love to you? For that matter, how can I say that I have ever been in love? It is such a relative thing. The love that applied the asp to Cleopatra's breast to me might be equal to that I offer a stray dog. Worse, the most insane, all-sacrificing passion that I was capable of might be dismissed as mere apathy if discovered in anyone else's heart. To expect, then, that the hypothetical object of my desire had reciprocal feelings which were exactly complementary was, purportedly, immature, misguided and mythical. I was neither an abject cynic because of this, nor a fanciful romantic. I was merely sadly, and very reluctantly, alone.

I tell you this, for I cannot hurt nor be hurt any more, in order to warn you of what is to come and how vicious it is. I realize I have digressed long enough, but I had to make myself clear in case you have any qualms or prudish inclinations or other such vices. For I believe, as I prepare to expose my trembling soul, that it is wise to ask the scarecrow if he is terrified of birds.

Part One

ROMANCE

The air is pure, as the kiss of a child, the sun is bright, the sky blue—what more does one want? What need have we here of passions, desires, regrets?

Lermontov: *A Hero of our Time*

1

My father died when I was eight years old. He was buried ten years later when his heart finally stopped beating. It was a merciful moment of departure for him and a bitter one for me. And that, really, is all that can be said about him, and all that I would ever want to say, without malice and without sadness, for that was the relationship we had. A man who was present at my conception, and I, eighteen years later, at his funeral. And yet, since I owe it to the amateur psycho-analyst in each of you to present at least a thumbnail sketch of my parents, though Aunt Sally is more what you have in mind, I will attempt a brief résumé, in which I will include at least one outrageous lie, and two rather endearing anagrams.

My father was born during the county of Essex. That is to say, his head (belly-button eyes, skin wrinkled like a tired balloon) emerged just outside Romford, and he was bottom-smacked into life on the outskirts of Southend. It was his first visit to the English seaside, and, blissfully, his last.

As I understood it, my grandfather had developed an insatiable penchant for Dan Leno, a music-hall entertainer, who was accustomed to perform (I think he sang and clowned) in a theatre in Southend every July and August. It was a permanent annual event my grandparents never missed and never wanted to, and that year was to be no exception, despite the fact that my father had been conceived (much to the lodger's surprise) on Guy Fawkes Day—it had rained heavily, the fireworks were ruined and my grandmother apparently was almost inconsolable.

Needless to say, this itinerant birth had a marked effect on my father, who never stayed in one place longer than he had to for the rest of his life. One hour after his fifteenth birthday, he collected his few possessions (one penknife, a cracked rotograph of his parents taken under duress, twenty-two shillings in gas shillings, and, romantic to the last, a copy of *Childe Harold* with somebody else's name in it), crept out into the night and never went home again. At least that is what I've been told, though I don't believe it, and nor should you; but, except for dragging in that incestuous lout Byron, I rather like the image. What I *do* know, is that seven years later my father was in Cairo and living with the first-floor maid of a wealthy Greek widow. 'I asked her', he told me once, having underestimated the *ouzo*, 'if her mistress was beautiful.' The maid, poor fool, had apparently shaken her head to the affirmative, being Greek too, and consequently found herself out of a job and on the way to ruin before she could say χαῖρετε νικῶμεν.

With his new wife, who was indeed wealthy and beautiful, my father honeymooned at the Shepheard's Hotel in Grand Style, leaving the suite only to shout abuse at the muezzin, whose incessant, though doubtless devoted, *Allah Akbar* disturbed not only his sunset, but also his sense of rhythm. Three and a half weeks of this was sufficient to drive both my parents out of Cairo, and north to Greece, stopping only at Alexandria, where my mother spent thirty-five minutes in a confessional, having been converted to Catholicism at an early age, perhaps, one surmises, because it was quieter.

I myself was born in Athens, in a convent hospital, and baptized a month later. I have a photo somewhere of a middle-aged woman in a cloche hat, standing outside a baroque church, clutching a blurred bundle, while a young man in his twenties, a white fedora hiding his eyes, hovers self-consciously in the background as if surprised to be there. He reminds one of one of those supernatural snapshots, so popular after the war, where dear, dead Auntie Lil appears bodyless, like the Cheshire Cat, grinning hideously and apparently inexplicably through a rather pert picture of Brighton Pavilion. If I had the baptismal photo at hand, I'd show it to you, not to demonstrate proof of my becoming a Child of Christ, but to show you the delicate face of my mother, and, more especially, her smile. I will never forget it. It was so exquisite, she only wore it on Grand Occasions (my baptism was one of them), and then it was her only jewellery.

When she died eight years later of cancer, her last words to my father were 'I love you', and then she smiled and returned, God willing, to heaven. It was the only cruel thing she ever did to my father, and he never forgave her. He was then only thirty years old, utterly alone, and with not a thing in the world he wanted to live for. Not even me.

* * *

I am sitting alone, hunched up on a cracked-leather seat, staring out at salmon-red mountains. The windows of the bus are spattered with red dust, stifling the stark light of the Adriatic, and the thick wired glass still bears torn reminders of black-out and smothered light. I am sitting alone, my hands clasped in my lap, aware of a constant monotone of Croatian from the passengers in front of me, as I gaze out at the empty land of Dalmatia.

A field of sunflowers bounces by on poor springs, and beyond that I catch a glimpse of deep azure, too dark to be sky; then the sea is below me and I swivel round in admiration, but it is gone, hidden by too tall cliffs, and I am in a forest of silent pines. An old woman on the next seat returns a stub of pencil to me. I take it with a half-smile, display it in my hand like the Holy Grail until she is sufficiently exhausted by her gesture and looks away, and then I drop it silently on the floor. It is wet with spittle and it isn't mine.

I am eighteen years old and sitting alone, crossing a land that is beautiful but unfamiliar to me, and therefore, unlike a woman, leaves no lingering impression other than a slight taste in the mouth and a blurred kaleidoscope of colour. The bus itself is even more forgettable, except that it is Lincoln pea green, has a metal Red Indian's head on the radiator as a motif (already its name is being mouthed by the more pedantic among you), and is unbearably hot and uncomfortable. I am sitting alone, a reluctant passenger, pressed in the rear corner seat with the debris of my journey littered around my shoes. I have spoken hardly a word to anybody for almost a week, being a poor linguist, and at first, aware of this deficiency, attempted to pass the hours by reading. However, never having acquired the extra concentration necessary for travelling, I abandoned *The Return of the Native* outside Winchester, before we'd hardly begun, to be joined in Paris by lesser meat (pornography of course, but remember I was still a virgin), and finally at Mantua, *An American Tragedy* was replaced, forsaken and unread, beneath folded pyjamas, and I resigned myself to the solitude of my own thoughts.

*   *   *

My aunt entered my bedroom suddenly, walked to the window and stared out at the grey sky, one hand abstract-

18

edly wiping away crumbs of earth spilled from a potted plant on the sill.

'Your father is dying,' she said, not turning round. 'Do you want to see him?'

'Where is he?'

'I'm not sure. I can't pronounce it but it begins with a Z.'

'Zanzibar?'

'No. No, I don't think it's Zanzibar ... '

Behind her back, I turn on my side and push the magazine safely away beneath my pillow.

*   *   *

I have never felt at ease in what is called a 'picture post-card town'. Somehow the combination of blue-ribboned prettiness and coy tradition usually associated with such a place induces in me a nausea I find hard to control. I long to urinate profusely over those coddled thatch-and-beams near the spinney, or scrawl multilingual obscenities on the slices of Roman pillar hidden in the olive grove. I poke out a mental tongue at the dead souls who inhabit such a sterile place, my right hand collecting yet another cheap pamphlet, my left hand dropping it immediately, in pieces, on reverently preserved flagstones. I am by no means a hardened cynic because of this, scorning the Romance of the Past. On the contrary, my aversion to the automated culture of the Present is legendary. I have always had a loathing for the impersonal landscape of today, and consider all men who profess an idolatry for a lifeless object, whether it be car, boat or rifle, to be socially very dull, and privately rather dangerous.

No—I am anything but cold towards my forebears. The shelves of my library sag under endless accounts of

Regency manners and Roman scandals, and, if you left me alone on the ploughed fields of Bosworth or Naseby, my imagination would run riot with sounds of hooves and visions of blood-stained lace. History has a living magic for me which needs only a rusted buckle or a yellowing canvas to stir the mind, and, at best, not even that. And so, I abhor the mummied shrine, elevated like a host by smug curators who offer it, seemingly intact (preserved daily by modern timber and stone), in order to attract the gaping tourist, half a crown in hand. It inflicts the same brutality on my senses as its living counterpart, the Professional Virgin, and so consequently is despicable. Zordar was such a place, ancient port of Dalmatia, cluttered with polished ruins, nodding peasants, and, as I was led to believe, the dying body of my father.

I arrived there at dawn, exhausted and despairing, and was abandoned immediately by the bus as it hurried away towards the south and the Greek border. Around me, fellow passengers chattered loudly and then wandered away to the sea edge in order to drop pebbles into the dark water, as if the journey had been merely a pilgrimage, and this action was the final ritual.

Then, when the sun finally cleared the vertebrae of islands strung out along the horizon, it was an hour later, and I was sitting asleep on a solitary bench (*In Loving Memory Of* and then a rectangle of brighter green betraying the broken plaque and its sad anonymity). The beach before me was deserted except for half a dozen wooden dinghies trembling above the tide as it eased them slowly off the pebbles.

'I don't think you ought to sleep there, boy. Not just there.'

I opened my eyes at the voice and squinted at the dark shape of a man (the sun was behind him) standing over me. He had spoken to me in English which surprised me, and was picking up my suitcase.

'It's very easy to see you are Henry's boy. The eyes ... My name is Miss Althaea. How do you do?'

Miss Althaea? I stood up and peered more closely. The light had been deceptive. I shook her hand, studying her face which was utterly hideous, and gave a hint of a smile.

The woman grinned back at me, then laughed openly, her enormous body shaking grotesquely under the black dress, as I looked self-consciously over her shoulder, struck by a sudden acute embarrassment.

'You're prettier than he is, boy,' she said finally, raising a hand and touching my cheek, 'and your skin is softer and rather hot.'

I turned away as a current of stale sweat reached my nostrils, and looked around helplessly for some form of escape, but Miss Althaea grabbed my arm and began to pull me along the beach.

'Come on, come on. There isn't much time,' and I am stumbling over the shifting stones, sometimes falling forward as she stops suddenly, my face banging against her shoulder, and I am being dragged (her grip is like a vice) between a row of stunted palm trees away from the dark core of the town.

'We must hurry. No delay. Already he might—'

'How is he?' I shout.

'No delay, boy. There isn't much time.'

I look for a rabbit hole.

*   *   *

Crumbling paving stones under my feet now. Scarlet sky over my head, a fritter of quaint buildings and quainter mountains to my left, and if I could see the Adriatic (which

I can't because of the massive bulk of this creature beside me) it would be on the right. Ahead, I can see a hotel. This gorgon beside me, of course, being more familiar with the area, sees *the* hotel, which seems destined to be our goal.

'Not much time, boy. Not much time. Hurry, hurry. Not much —'

After a further five minutes of exhaustive running, we arrived at the entrance to the building, and there finally, blissfully, the woman stopped. I collapsed unashamedly on to the low tiled wall before the hotel, and sat, chest heaving, staring down at the dry sand beneath my feet. The suitcase was placed between my legs, and I heard her say:

'Wait there, boy. I'll see if he is still alive,' and then she was gone, leaving only the acrid smell of sweat behind her. Who she was I didn't know, nor, at the time, did I care. Possibly a nurse to my father, or a housekeeper. A mistress? Good God, I should hope not.

Ten minutes passed and Miss Althaea hadn't returned, and so, feeling reasonably recovered from the ordeal, I stood up and looked around. The hotel itself lay on the foreshore, cut off from the main part of the town and linked by a single road, a mere dust track, that had rebelled from the main coast route two miles before Zordar, then had run along the beach to split the town, take in the hotel and, finally repentant, rejoin the highway at the edge of the surrounding forest. There were no other buildings of any kind, neither church nor house, within a mile radius of the hotel, and what there was, was mere scrub or sand or palm tree.

The building itself was rather baroque in appearance, full of curlicues and wrought-iron roses, coloured tiles and carved gables, and was not unpleasing to look at. I was told later that the poet Rimbaud had stayed there once, in a fourth-floor room, and that the Archduke Ferdinand himself had first made love to his wife in the Peacock Suite, which was hardly in its favour. The hotel was called The Beograd.

Fifteen minutes went by, and still that woman had not reappeared. I walked back a few yards and stared up at the windows as if to discover some kind of sign or light, but all the windows were dark or shuttered, and the only noise came from the sea and the cooks in the kitchen preparing early breakfast.

Hesitating only long enough to straighten my clothes and slick down my hair (I was as misguidedly vain then as I am now), I approached the entrance to the hotel, walked up the steps and pushed open the doors into the foyer. I hadn't travelled fifteen hundred miles to be abandoned in the middle of nowhere, when my father was almost certainly at death's door, and when I myself was anxious to find a toilet before it was too late. The lobby lived up to the extravagant decor of the exterior, and seemed to be entirely composed of enormous mirrors and shiny gold cherubs with bottom faces. A chandelier the size of a Thames buoy hung from the ceiling, and portraits of medieval princes filled whatever area of wall was still left opaque. But I would be deceiving you if I were to give you the impression that this set-piece was all I saw when I pushed through those glass doors. No, that would be false. For to tell you the truth, I never noticed the room at all, not a bit of it, and it wasn't till much later that I was aware of even the slightest hint of a mirror, or the merest touch of a cherub. I saw nothing but a girl, sitting on a rather delicate and very, very lucky chaise-longue in the corner.

She was perhaps fourteen or fifteen, no more, and sat, her thin hands clasped carefully one within the other, thumbs crossed, resting on her lap. Her body was leaning forward as if she was looking over an imaginary wall or counting deceptive goldfish in a pond, and her blonde hair hung straight and long, dropping eighteen inches from beneath a large hat to complete the triangle of her pose, and rest on her bare knees. She wore a white dress with bunched sleeves and blue embroidery on the hem, along the waist, around the neck and, I believe, across the back of the shoulder. The design of the dress was deceptive at that angle but it seemed to be shaped deliberately around the bodice (my euphemism is merely to calm my own excitement, not to tease yours), and then to flair out at the waist in a series of folds (I counted fourteen in the front), till it reached the hem and the band of neat embroidery. A blue ribbon, half an inch in width, was threaded through the yoke of the dress, and two further ribbons, a third of an inch wider, encircled the rim of the sleeves at the bicep. There was a small coffee stain, the size of a sixpence, on the solar plexus of the dress.

On her head was a circular hat made of straw, and resembling a rather large boater. The band was blue to match the ribbons in the dress, but a darker blue, similar to the colour on the back of some matchboxes. Her legs were parallel to each other, touching and bent at the knees, then angling back under the chaise-longue so that her ankles returned to the main weight of the body, and her whole pose resembled the letter S endearingly angled.

On her feet were a pair of white shoes, rather dirty at the toe, buttoned with a thin strap over the instep. The girl herself was rather thin and with a fair skin which was neatly sun-tanned on the legs and arms, but the nose was peeling pink, and so was a little of her chin. The face itself was pretty in repose, though more attractive by its innocence than by its design. Her eyes, I think, were blue.

As I gazed at her, I heard the doors behind me swing

back into place, and the girl raised her head slightly without glancing around, and I knew that all I ever wanted to do, whatever happened, was to own her, to pick her up and clip her into my inside pocket next to my ball-point pen. That's how innocent it was. But if I only knew then what I know now, I would have run out of that foyer, run out into the mountains, into the sea, anywhere, anywhere but in that mirrored limbo with that child. I wanted her then—oh yes, openly, naively, and with all the absurd gentleness of my age—and it was the cruellest thing I ever did. If I had died five minutes before, if the bus had not stopped, if this angelic child hadn't sat in the foyer, I wouldn't have committed the hell I did, and finally, twenty years later, when all seemed madness, I wouldn't have tied a rope around my neck and jumped trembling into the void. It was as tragic as that.

The coffee stain, by the way, turned out to be tea. *Much* easier to clean.

I don't know how long I stood and stared at her, my mind desperately phrasing absurd introductions, but not once did she speak, nor look in my direction, nor make any sign that she knew of my presence. She just sat there, quite still, gazing at the floor. Relieved from the fear that I might be observed, though somewhat disappointed by her apathy, I studied each facet of her pose in the mirrors around me (left profile, right profile, petit-point scar above the elbow), as if she were a precious stone or a rare orchid on display. Which, in a way, she was. May I make it clear that no thoughts of intimacy of any kind crossed my mind, not because of my age or my inexperience (I had mentally dry-runned the sexual act a thousand times since puberty), but simply because I had been taught that even to con-template such a desire was evil and could only lead me to

25

hell. I was only eighteen and terrified of being damned. You see how indoctrinated I already was—I even had a silver crucifix hanging round my neck, dammit. On a chain.

Doubts were already there of course, and lusts, but not as strong, not in any way as strong as my desire to be one of the chosen. *Denial of the erection to obtain the election* ran a witless graffiti on the back pew of the chapel. Of course, I tried to justify my urges by devious means, and at the age of seventeen in a blinding flash of agnosticism, I had written in a notebook: 'Jesus Christ must have experienced sex in some form or other. Just because he had to endure a Virgin Birth didn't mean he had to suffer a Virgin Death as well.' On reading it next day, I trembled and went white and burnt it immediately, too guilty even to confess it that afternoon. I remember it took me three months and half a bottle of Moselle to absolve my soul finally of the stain. I received six Hail Mary's as a penance, and thanked God it was not the pilgrimage to Damascus I expected. My schizophrenia had begun that early.

I sat down in the foyer opposite the girl and a little to her right, my nose pointing at a talentless oil of Charles the Bold, my eyes straying constantly to the chaise-longue.

Suddenly there was a whirr of machinery and the rattling of cables, and I became aware that two of the mirrors represented the doors of a lift. As I turned towards them curiously (the girl didn't move a muscle. Was her father a taxidermist, by any chance?), the two doors slid slowly apart to reveal the obscene figure of Miss Althaea, looking rather breathless and strangely preoccupied. She came out of the lift, closing the inner metal gates behind her, gazed round the foyer and rested her eyes on the girl. Much to my surprise I saw her walk slowly to the chaise-longue and sit down in an identical pose and light a cigarette. No indication of her action was registered on the girl's face until the older woman bent over and whispered in the other's ear, and then both of them looked across the room in my direction. It was only a glance lasting a second and utterly uninvolved, like that of a casual tourist being shown yet another museum piece—look, confirmation, dismissal. And yet there was something sinister about it, as if I myself were part of a plan set in motion before my arrival. I have no idea why I felt that, but I remember I blushed crimson at the thought and contemplated the buckled shoes of Maximilian the First.

I could sense the scrutiny continuing from across the room, then suddenly I heard a high, light pizzicato of laughter, which could only have come from the girl. It echoed round the foyer, increasing in volume, an almost insane tremolo, higher and higher, wave upon wave, until abruptly it stopped and the lift doors slammed shut and she was gone. Slowly, I forced myself to turn and saw that Miss Althaea remained, relighting a new cigarette from the old.

'He's asleep, boy,' she said as if nothing had happened.

'Who?' I replied.

'Your father.'

'Oh.' And then adding as if to recompense my initial callousness, 'Can I see him now?'

Miss Althaea stubbed out the cigarette and walked across the magenta carpet towards me, and studied me carefully, her head at an angle, hands on hips.

'Have you wondered what relationship I have with him, boy?'

'Nurse?' I ventured gallantly.

'Lover,' she replied.

I nodded idiotically and pulled down the cuffs of my shirt.

'It's because I'm ugly, you see,' she continued. 'That's

the only reason. He only wants the monsters and the cripples, boy. People like that. No one pretty, no one appealing. Just the monsters and cripples … '

Her voice trailed away and I sneaked a glance up at her. She was looking out through the glass doors at the early morning light and the trees at the foot of the mountains. Her expression was painfully sad, if any expression could be discerned on those grotesque sagging cheeks. Unable to say anything, I stood up in order to leave her alone, but she seized my arm, and pulled me close to her, thrusting her face into mine. I winced as she breathed over me.

'He doesn't want to risk finding someone more beautiful than her, boy. Someone more … lovely than her. Don't you know that? She's been dead ten years now, but he couldn't bear … he couldn't stand to discover that someone might be better. He couldn't bear it, you see, boy. I know that. I can tell … '

I felt vomit rising in my gullet as I strained to avoid the stink from her mouth.

'Monsters and cripples, boy,' she repeated. 'Like me.'

'Why can't I see him now?'

'Because he's asleep. He said he will see you this afternoon when he's rested.'

'Why this afternoon and not now?'

'That's what he wants, boy. This afternoon … '

'Supposing he dies before … '

'No. He knows when he will die.'

And then she released me and walked to the glass doors and pushed them open, stopping only to say:

'*She* wants you, boy. She does.'

Automatically I look at the empty chaise-longue but make no reply. I am conscious of sweat.

'Monsters and cripples, boy,' Miss Althaea repeated

once more and left. I watched her waddle down the steps and on to the pale-red sand of the road, then turn and walk out of sight behind the building.

I found myself alone once more in the silence of the foyer. '*She* wants you. She does' reverberated in my mind, and I count the portraits on the walls (eight) and observe my flushed reflection in the gilded mirrors. My fingers caress the cold face of a cherubim as I walk deliberately, despite myself, to the chaise-longue in the corner. It lies below me, the seat on a par with my knees, its deep velvet covering edged in silk. I stare down at it, my heart racing, my ears straining for any alien sound, and then slowly, slowly I lower my right hand face down towards the very spot where the girl had sat. The gentle depression, the size of a Sunday dinner-plate, is still there. My palm touches the soft velvet, hovering anxiously for a moment above it, then descending cautiously till it touches, and I spread my fingers and my hand deep into the delicate concave moulded so recently by the girl. It is still warm. I immediately snatch my scorched hand away and run feverishly without looking back, across the foyer, out of the hotel and into the blinding sunlight, not stopping until I feel the beach under my feet, and the water lapping at my shoes. I have remembered the priests and feel desperately ashamed.

2

To say that my life until the age of eighteen was sheltered is nothing more than a gross understatement. Remember, I was virtually an orphan (having been abandoned by my father at the age of eight), and consequently open house to all the influences and demands, good or bad, of my guardians and teachers.

At nine, I had been packed off to an austere boarding school in England, and I was to remain in such a place till my eighteenth birthday. I will not dwell on the unhappiness and the frustrations I endured there, but may I say that of all the many people I have met in my life (short though it was), there are few more bigoted, more unsophisticated and ultimately more tasteless than the products of the English public school. If that sounds like a bigoted, unsophisticated and tasteless generalization, remember my education. Fortunately, for my own integrity and also for my own physical make-up, I broke the traditional link (public school, Oxbridge, the Guards) after the first stage, and so managed, at least, to keep my sexual impulses free from the customary post-prep gropings of boy upon boy, grub upon grub. For I learnt very early on, that if the spotty-faced Nigel in the next dorm doesn't get you in the school, he'll get you, ten years later, in the barracks.

I was, of course, in my life, hardly a very handsome man to look at. The photos you saw of my later years (*Paris Match*, I think, featured a rather deft study in colour to illustrate a somewhat vicious critique of my character) showed me to be physically quite unremarkable, and except for stunning blue eyes—never appreciated by the newspaper reader—facially rather plain. At eighteen, I was even more unattractive, being extraordinarily thin and painfully gauche. I was also unskilful in that lecherous art for which I was condemned, and condemned unjustifiably may I add. But more of that later.

I say all this to show you my state of mind as I stood on that deserted beach on the Adriatic, unaware of the agonizing events that were to take place before the day was out.

With the hotel behind me, standing on a low wooden jetty, I could see the shallow string of islands decorating the horizon. Most of them seemed little more than half a mile in length, though my estimates were by no means accurate. It was a clear day and by now very hot, and the shapes of trees and rocks could easily be distinguished against the azure sky. As I stared across the water, I suddenly had an absurd urge to hire a boat and sail out to the islands and explore. It was now only ten in the morning, and there seemed nowhere else to go (the town itself was much too far away and somewhat uninviting), and besides, the prospect of being alone, cut off from civilization, was very appealing.

I would first have to find a boat, but that didn't appear to present too great a problem, as there were at least a dozen within a few yards of me. Stimulated by this adventure, I turned and hurried back along the jetty towards the shore, pulling off my heavy tweed jacket and loosening my tie, and jumped down on to the beach. On approaching close to the boats, I noticed to my disappointment that they were all rowboats and dinghies, and much bigger than I imagined. It was out of the question, of course, to think of taking one of these, since I was hardly strong enough or even experienced enough to cover the distance from here to the islands on a pair of oars alone.

I began, then, to wander along the tide-edge, expecting to find a motor boat or a small yacht round each corner, but after a mile of frustrated searching, the chances seemed remote. My shirt, by now, was under my arm inside my jacket, and I could feel the sun burning into my shoulders and on to the back of my neck and through my hair. The pebbles on the beach had been left behind long ago, and I now walked on sand or rock, jumping over hidden pools or climbing low balconies of pink cliff. At one point, I stopped and looked about me, and was surprised to find myself utterly alone (an evergreen malady I was rarely without), and almost certainly lost. I hadn't seen a boat for an hour or more, not of any kind, and my chances of reaching the islands appeared almost hopeless. I imagined, by the lack of shadow, it was about noon, and I was reminded of the ache in my stomach.

Ahead, I could see only more miles of rock and an occasional tree, and there seemed nothing for it but to return the way I had come. I was hungry, exhausted and very hot, and would, at the drop of anyone's hat, have gladly stripped off my remaining clothes and plunged naked into the sea. Unfortunately, I was not only ridiculously shy (and still am), I was also no exhibitionist. In fact, wanton exposure of my assets to all and sundry never did become a penchant of mine, and till the day I died, I retained a Victorian antipathy for the purse-mouthed poseur. Exhibitionism is a feminine trait, for the basic reason that women are proud of their bodies, and wish them to be seen, adorned or unadorned, depending on inclination. Men, on the other hand, generally have no such whim. Not because they are ashamed of reckless exposure, but simply because they find such a state to be

32

not only uncomfortable, but also pointless. Naturally, I cannot speak for the homosexual fop, or the wretched little drag, or even for that unzipped old man by the hockey field, since fortunately I was never one of them, though the latter almost became a reality in my last miserable months.

And so, respectable and stupid to the last, I turned to amble towards the hotel, wilting under the heat, and then stopped dead. No more than five or six yards in front of me, kneeling on the sand, was the girl in the white dress. She was still wearing it, though it had become rather grubbier than before, and there was a small tear on the left sleeve. She had her back to me, her head bent forward, and resembled the earlier pose to such a degree that I feared it was her only one. Her hat lay near her, and I could see all her hair, the colour of saffron, as it hung from its central parting. Surprised by this encounter, and, I must admit, slightly perturbed (I assumed she had appeared from out of that wood over there), I pulled on my shirt again and walked slowly towards her.

After two steps, I realized that she was, in fact, writing with her forefinger in the sand. It looked like a word, rather large and not unfamiliar. Drawn by this, I found myself almost on top of her, and looking over her shoulder. There were seven letters in all, etched out deep in the sand, and each about a foot in height. Suddenly, the girl, conscious of my intrusion, feverishly scrubbed out the writing, digging her nails into the ground to obliterate the word and hide it from my gaze. But it was too late, for I had already seen it and no amount of sand could blot it out of my mind. The word she had written so carefully and so forcefully, was my own name.

*   *   *

'A likely story, sir.'
'How do you know, Catesby? I hadn't met you then!'
'No, sir. Shall I run your bath now?'
'You know I never take baths in the morning.'
'Then shall I run your shaving mug?'
'But you are dead too, Catesby, aren't you? Catesby? Catesby?'

*   *   *

The girl got up and stood on the churned sand, brushing
the sand away from her dress and off her bare legs. She
was about five foot six inches in height, no less, with a
good body for her age, though rather small breasted and
slightly bow-legged. Her nose was small and straight,
finely etched, and her eyes were unnaturally large and
wide-spaced. Her eyebrows complimented her face, as
eyebrows usually do. Little else can be said about eyebrows. On her left shin was a slight graze, as if she had
just knocked it against a rock or against a low wall. I
discovered later that it was in fact caused by her shoe.

'You won't find a boat here,' she said, screwing up her
eyes against the sun. Her voice was quite pleasant, though
rather ill at ease in public. It was obviously designed to ask
such things as the meaning of '*spätlese*' or the correct way
to pronounce 'mnemonic', and was at its best only on the
telephone or on the pillow. I was enchanted.

'I've been following you all morning,' she continued, 'ever
since you left the hotel. You didn't notice me, did you?'

'No,' I replied, utterly confused, buttoning up my shirt
and dropping my jacket.

The girl laughed and then suddenly ran straight down
the beach and into the sea, not stopping till the water was
around her waist. I watched her in amazement, her hat by
my feet. The waves churned around her, some of them the

height of her shoulders and in no time she was soaked to the skin, the dress swirling limply about her legs and her hair hanging darker now, licked to her face. I began to walk down the beach towards her, hypnotized by the scene, and as I approached I could hear her voice singing above the waves, though the words were unrecognizable and the tune erratic. A sudden chill ran down me, for no reason, as if I were anticipating something as yet unknown, and I became more convinced than ever that all this — the beach, the girl, the singing, my presence — was pre-destined, and worse, that it was only the beginning. I immediately shrugged off the thought as being morbid fantasy. I have always had a pathetically vivid imagination which has often entertained me for hours on end, and so I was well aware, even at eighteen, how unreliable it was.

The girl was before me now, half-submerged in the surf, her head turned away from me, as she waded even deeper into the sea. I could still hear her voice, and my ears strained to catch a word, a line of the song. I walked towards her till I too was in the tide, and then I heard the words clearly for the first time. Surprisingly, they were familiar, though I failed to recognize their origin immediately.

'Not a flower, not a flower sweet,'

she sang, her voice high and clear.

'Not a friend, not a friend greet
My poor corse, where my bones shall be thrown.'

More distant now as the water reached her chin, stifled as it plunged over her head.

'A thousand thousand sighs to save,
Lay me, O! where
Sad true lover never—'

Horrified, I finally recognized the song. It was originally sung by Ophelia before she drowned herself. Immediately, I am running blindly into the sea, stumbling on the shifting sand, hurrying towards her against the current, and my arms are around her waist as she slides beneath the waves, and I begin to pull her back towards the shore. She doesn't struggle. I lay her down beside her hat, and carefully remove wet strands of hair from her forehead and eyes, and cover her knees with the hem of her dress. A triangle of red varnish still clings defiantly to the second toe of her right foot. Fortunately, I am relieved to find she is still alive, as the rhythmic swell of her baby breasts teases me under the wet bodice. I have saved her life (*Will God now save mine?*) though I am not sure she wanted me to.

After a moment, she opens her eyes and sits up.

'Why did you do that?'

'I thought you were going to drown,' I reply.

'Why did you think that? Why did you think I was going to drown?'

I immediately turn away, and begin to walk back along the beach. I have just remembered that it wasn't Ophelia at all who sang that song. It was that damn clown in *Twelfth Night* (of all people), who probably bit-played his life till he was ninety.

Behind me, I hear the girl running after me and then she is by my side. We reach the edge of the wood and I can see the hotel.

'Let us go to the island,' the girl is saying. 'I know where there is a boat.'

I feel the sun already drying my clothes, though I ought to remove my shoes.

'I'm sorry,' I reply. 'What did you say?'

*   *   *

My father is dying. He lies, at the age of forty, in his quilted death-bed in one of the rooms of that hotel on the beach. The boat I am in pulls farther and farther away from the shore, and in the bow, a girl in a white dress lies perfectly still, face down, one hand trailing in the water. The only sound is the deep chug of the outboard motor, and ahead of me I can see three islands easing up to meet me. My father is dying, and I feel almost nothing.

*   *   *

The boy slowly realized that she was watching him, that she had turned over and sat up and was watching him from the other side of the boat. He could feel her gaze on his cheek, and on the right side of his neck just above the collar. For a futile moment, he tried to concentrate on the foam churning out from under the rudder, framing it and hanging it on a wall, in order to avoid turning towards her. But he had to look round, if only to discover the direction they were going and the state he was in.

And so he turned towards her, casually at first, his eyes deliberately aimed safely over her head; then more boldly, dropping his gaze down an octave of sky until the first millimetre of her head appeared just beneath his line of vision. And then finally, panning his eyes in a smooth downward arc until her face dominated the frame, except for a triangle of blue sky by her right cheek, where her hair had been blown back by the breeze.

It was her tongue he noticed first. It was the colour of an open pomegranate, a rich Roman red, as if she had held it between thumb and forefinger and dipped it in wine. The tip itself was more pointed than is usual, and even more luscious in colour, and was now resting idly in the outer corner of her mouth. As he watched, she slid it slowly along the dry underside of her upper lip, wetting the skin and leaving, for a brief second, a glistening cobweb of saliva between upper and lower lip, and then coyly drew it back out of sight. But only for an instant, as she allowed it to force its way gently between her teeth once more, easing them apart, before it lingered again, moist and firm, in the same corner, against her cheek. The whole action was accompanied by the innocence of her gaze, as she stared, not *at* the boy, but through him, through his eyes and into his mind, and out on to the horizon.

For a full minute, the small boat drifted aimlessly in the water, its rudder forgotten by the boy, as he sat mesmerized in the stern, his cheeks stained the same colour as the inside of the girl's mouth. An unexpected gust of wind from the west suddenly broke the trance, as it caught the boat by its tail and shook it, causing some water to spill over its port side and soak the shoes and socks of one of the passengers, and cleanse the bare feet of the other.

It need hardly be said, of course, that the girl had seventeen hooks attached to seventeen eyes running the full length of the spine of her dress.

3

The island was smaller than I thought, a mere half a mile across, so that one could easily tour it in an hour and still have time to contemplate the eucalyptus or leave one's surname on a rock. It appeared to be mostly foliage (fern, briar) clinging to the feet of a dense wood. The trees ran right down to the sea itself, and except for a strip of beach (more rock than sand) were partly submerged by the water. There appeared to be no sign of life, neither person nor even animal, and the whole area seemed to be like some form of limbo in the ocean, very hot and very still.

As soon as we had pulled the boat on to the small and only beach, Antonella (for that was her name) walked away into the trees without looking back, and left me alone. By this time I had become—I was going to say 'accustomed' but it's hardly the word—*drugged* by Antonella's behaviour, and no longer surprised by it. The truth is, however, that I was indeed hypnotized. Ridiculous as it may seem, I felt as if I were a mere pawn to her wishes, a spellbound thing, incapable of resisting, and not wanting to. I was infatuated by her and in her power, and that is all I can say. And if there is any among you who have never experienced that emotion, even for a second, then I trust you are in the kindergarten where you belong. Or in the kennel.

At first, I thought I would explore, but conscious more than ever of the heat, and even more of the absence of Antonella, I decided to follow her.

I am not alone, I am sure, in finding the sun a strong aphrodisiac, especially if inflicted upon a youth of my age, wilting under the pressure of tweeds, outrageous sexual curiosity, and the near-by presence of a sorceress. I am not excusing my subsequent behaviour, nor even justifying it. I am merely amusing myself by adding a little embroidery here and there. Besides, the whole situation (deserted island, hot sun, hotter girl) was too much like one of my more restrained masturbatory fantasies to avoid being tinged with acute sexual arousal on my part. I had never seen a woman completely naked, except in two dimension, nor even rested my hand on a breast or a thigh. The schooling that professed to have broadened my mind only narrowed it by denying me not only the right to revisit the womb, but even to recognize it if I got there. The grubby drawings in the school toilet could never have offered me an accurate illustration, since the female organ (unlike the baroque possibilities of the male) is hardly, by itself, the most practical Still Life, especially for the wretched sculptor. Consequently, it has to be accompanied, in those tiled graffiti, by bold pencil flourishes of buttock and leg (much simpler to draw), and perhaps a navel or two. It is never successful on its own. My curiosity therefore was natural, and I was now anxious to rekindle it once more, encouraged by the unreality of the mood. Anxious that is, until I realized I was lost.

One tree looks just like another if you haven't seen it before, and though the wood wasn't very thick, the irritation of foliage around my ankles and low-hanging leaves across my face failed to encourage my search. Now and again, I caught a glimpse of the sea through a branch or over a low bush, though I hardly needed the sight of it to remind me it was there, since nowhere on the island could one avoid hearing the constant sigh of wave upon wave, surf upon sand.

I suppose I must have walked for about half an hour (though, curiously, time is deceptive when one is on foot), and had gone so far as to remove my shirt once more, and would have removed my shoes too except for the fact that I wondered about snakes. Suddenly, I emerged on to a clearing, and found that I had actually been walking up-hill, for below me now was sea and a row of low trees. I was on a smooth shelf of rock, stretching across the island, then disappearing under the water to reappear on another island about a mile away. About forty feet to my right, the rock dropped sharply out of sight, presumably to the sea.

Realizing that from this height there was a good chance I might see the whereabouts of Antonella, I began to walk along the surface of the shelf towards the edge. Halfway across, my eye was caught by something white, a bird perhaps, huddled beneath a dry gorse to my left. At first, it seemed to move, to struggle, as if wounded or caught in a trap. But then as I approached I realized that it was the wind that disturbed it, and that it wasn't a bird at all, or any animal of any kind. It was in fact a dress, rather dirty and decorated in blue ribbon, lying discarded by the edge of the rock.

I froze immediately, stunned by the realization of what might have happened, and as if to anticipate my actions, a freak gust of wind dived and caught the dress, and in one blow flicked it into the air, billowing it out, then dropped it over the rim towards the rocks below. Fearing the worst, I hurried to the edge and peered over. About twenty feet below me, a narrow chin of rock jutted out from the main face, and formed a balcony the size of a small room.

I saw her immediately, stretched out along this narrow ledge. She was lying stomach down, her head on one side, facing out to the horizon, her hair pillowing her cheek and caressing her shoulders. She was hugging the smooth surface of the rock like a lizard or a large cat, arms and legs spreadeagled, and was not only quite still but also quite naked. I had the impression that she was asleep, but no one could be sure at that distance. She may well have been merely daydreaming.

*   *   *

There should be twenty-four pieces of jigsaw altogether in your box, so we would advise you to count them now before we begin. There is nothing worse than holding up everybody else while you hunt for a piece of sky down the back of the Knole sofa, just when the finished masterpiece is in sight. Moreover, we want to remind you once more to read the writing on the lid carefully, and to note that the completed puzzle forms a rectangle of at least five feet six inches by three foot three inches. So, you see, nothing less than a room cleared of lamps and coffee tables, or a full-sized billiard table will do. One might, of course, get away with it on the kitchen floor, but only if you lock Bonzo in the toolshed, or leave him with the neighbours round the corner. Muddy paws can create havoc with the design.

Assuming, then, that you are ready, let us begin, but remember there are no prizes for the winner—not even a certificate. You will treat it merely as a *divertissement*.

Now, you will notice that the colours grey and beige feature a great deal on the numbered pieces, and since this is a mystery puzzle, we will give you a clue by telling you that the colour 'grey' represents rock, and the colour 'beige' represents skin. For example, piece Number 5 depicts a female shoulder and a tiny piece of neck, piece Number 22 is a right foot underside up, and piece Number 14, which is a slightly lighter beige, is a small and rather delicate bottom. This last piece is usually stolen and made into a badge.

When the whole puzzle is completed (and it shouldn't take you longer than fifteen minutes), you will find lying under your feet a painting of a young girl with blonde hair, who appears to be asleep on a rock, and not, as you first suspected, on the back of an elephant. The picture is not unlike a calendar study, or a pin-up, except for her remarkable back, which you have no doubt noticed. It is nothing less than exquisite. A wide triangular plain below the neck, disturbed only slightly by the suggestion of shoulder blades and the whimper of a spine, then narrowing to the waist, the skin stretched taut so that if one laid one's hand against it, one could feel the ripple of the ribs under the fingers with only the slightest pressure; and then, continuing to rise and curve round soft hips that cry out to be decorated—small, firm, almost boyish and yet uniquely feminine. Eve had such a bottom. So did Messalina. And so did that rather vain señorita who took off her knickers and posed with cherub and mirror for Velasquez.

The title of the puzzle-painting you have just made is 'On First Seeing Antonella Naked', and is very rare. The original belonged to a playboy, whose name we have forgotten, but who died quite recently. It is not as you see a brilliant piece of work, as apparently it was painted from a verbal description of the owner's. We ourselves have manufactured it as a puzzle, because of our admiration, as we have said before, for the girl's body, expecially as seen from the rear. In fact, the late owner himself once made quite an amusing joke about it, by saying that he was sure the main reason the Iceni chose Boadicea to lead them, was because she had such a beautiful back. We believe those were his words.

The picture, by the way, was painted by someone called Cotesby. Or is it *Ca*tesby?

*   *   *

She wasn't asleep. That was evident almost immediately. She wasn't even daydreaming, or admiring the view. She was in fact waiting for me. I never discovered this till much later, when the whole thing was over and I was cowering within myself, wallowing in my own vomit.

Of course, at the beginning, I couldn't resist her, and nor could you, and even though I was trembling uncontrollably (partly through anticipation, but mostly through fear), I climbed down to the narrow ledge of grey rock, and allowed her to evacuate my soul. And even though my body catapulted violently when her hand first touched my skin, and her fingers first explored the buckle of my belt, I couldn't stop myself from reaching down to discover for the first time the feel of damp hair in the palm of my hand. Of course I was inadequate. All the words in the world couldn't describe the bitter frustration of that. I will not attempt to excuse my clumsiness nor my sickening lack of control, nor even my selfish scrabbling of breast and hair, for I shudder even now to recall it. I was not just losing my innocence on that hot afternoon, I was also beginning to lose my life.

It must have been about four o'clock when I became aware of this, when the shadows were growing long and the detumescence was almost complete. I remember her under me, her teeth having just drawn blood from my shoulder, and that I had become conscious of severe grazes on each of my elbows. I remember I was no longer inside her, but angled more across her, at right angles, my hips on the rock and my chest pressed on to her stomach. I was aware of Antonella smiling almost mockingly at me, and of her own hand caressing her right breast lovingly, her thumb and forefinger squeezing the nipple back and forth as if she were winding a watch. I remember too that I was looking over the edge of the ledge, and that I could see the white dress once more, clinging to the branches of a tree below me, and that I suddenly realized that that was all she could have been wearing.

I seem to recall a hundred more things about that moment—the sun burning my back, the gentle moaning from Antonella as she teased herself, the sudden appearance of a group of red ants from out of the rock, the noise of the sea, the low rumble of my empty stomach. But there is one thing I remember above all else, and I could never forget. I remember noticing the crucifix around my neck for the first time since it began, and feeling not only desperately ashamed (I was already that), but sickeningly frightened. I had sinned. I had defied the laws of God and I had sinned. I had committed it mortally and my soul was black. If I died then, I would go to hell, for that was what I had been taught and that was what I believed. I could never ever expect God to hear me until I was cleansed once more. I was a grub, a base thing. A sore. I had sinned and it was the most terrifying moment of my life.

As if to strengthen my own fear, I felt that the very trees below me and the sky above were pressing me down, threatening me with revenge. Even the rock face itself seemed to loom closer over me, until in panic I threw myself away from the flesh that contaminated me, and clung to the cliff, digging my nails into the rock, in order to save myself from spinning down on to the rocks below and the hell beneath.

Antonella seemed oblivious of the crime, for she simply yawned and turned over on to her stomach like the slug she was. I don't know how I managed to dress on that narrow ledge, crammed between the edge and that whore, but I did, though covering my nakedness in no way helped to cover my sickening guilt.

Then suddenly it happened. Quietly at first, then increasing in volume, a steady throbbing that seemed to reverberate throughout the island. It sounded somewhat like a swarm of bees, but more human, more alive, and much more terrifying.

'Can't you hear it?' I whispered anxiously, my mouth dry.

But Antonella only lifted her shoulders in an apathetic shrug and scratched the base of her spine.

'Listen!' I cried, frightened to raise my voice. 'Surely you must hear it?'

It was incessant now, a driving buzz, swelling over and over, just above my head. It pounded in my ears and through my brain, and no matter how much I pressed my hands to my head, the sound was there, louder and more strident every second.

Suddenly, I could bear it no longer, and in one frightened motion I stood up and raised my head towards the clifftop, opening my mouth to scream at the evil that was surely there. But no sound hit the air, for my mouth froze half-open as I saw the hunched shapes above me. There were eight of them, all identically dressed, their black clothes and bowed heads silhouetted against the deepening sky. They were chanting in unison, over and over again, and in their hands each clutched a long, hand-carved wooden rosary.

'Nuns,' I heard Antonella murmur. 'Just nuns.'

*   *   *

Halfway across the water, I noticed that some of the lights in the hotel had been switched on, though most of the windows were shuttered.

'All the islands round here are inhabited by nuns. Didn't you know that? Everybody knows that. Even me.'

She then chewed at a piece of loose fingernail and spat it out over the side of the boat. She was sitting on the centre plank seat, facing me, her right leg bent under her, her dress (the tree was child's play) once more in its place. From where I sat at the rudder, I could see under the hem and if I slumped a bit lower, like this, I could even catch a glimpse of bare thigh and a hint of stomach.

'No one else is allowed on them at all,' she continued, frowning at a piece of dirt discovered between her toes. 'It's forbidden. They belong to God, you see. God. Him up there. You can't even *walk* on them, let alone ... '

She giggles and I close my eyes tightly. My temperature is rising again, despite myself, and now I know I am surely damned. I would gladly capsize this boat now and drown us both, except that I have never been over-fond of Shelley.

I hear her laugh once more and I envy my father.

*   *   *

When we reached the mainland, Miss Althaea was there to meet us and take me back to the hotel. She made no comment, nor in a look or a gesture did she indicate any surprise at Antonella and I being together. I must admit I was grateful for that.

It was now almost dark, though still very warm, and I could hear other people moving about in the hotel, or strolling out on to the terrace to see if the sea was still there.

The beach itself appeared to be deserted at first, until I noticed a man standing about fifty yards away, looking in my direction. Normally, I wouldn't have taken too much notice of this, but I was struck by something vaguely familiar about him, something strangely intimate, as if he were a long lost twin or somebody's brother to whom I had been introduced on a favourite Sports' Day. He must have been about thirty years old, tall, and wearing what appeared to be a plain, dark, three-piece suit. I could see blurred flashes of his shirtcuffs in the gloom, and something brittle and shining in his right hand, which I realized was a knife. As I gazed at him, he turned his head away until he was in profile (aquiline nose, absurd classical eyes, the mouth of a marquis), and idly concentrated his attention on peeling the orange in his left hand, whittling the peel into a brilliant curlicue that spun lazily beneath the fruit before dropping silently, and a little reluctantly, to the ground.

My attention was distracted from this slightly sinister scene by the sound of an orchestra from a window above me. The music was obviously coming from a record player or a radio, and I remember it distinctly even now because I knew the tune well. At the age of thirteen, I and another boy in my class (Roger Chaffinch) had begun collecting the records of Artie Shaw, the popular clarinettist, and I had become especially fond of one in particular called 'I've Got You Under My Skin' (Parlophone R.3042). It was this very record that was being played above me, and may I say it still sounded rather nostalgic despite my paranoic mood, though perhaps there was a little too much treble for comfort.

'Come along, boy, come along. It's time now,' I heard Miss Althaea say, and I nodded and hurried after her. But not before glancing back towards the beach. The man, whoever he was, had, of course, disappeared.

At the foyer, Antonella left us without a word, and I can't say I was sorry to see her go, though my eyes did stray to the back of her legs and to my own discordant attempt to fasten the back of her dress.

'I'll leave you here now, boy. You go to him on your own. Third floor.'

And the monster too was gone and I was left alone.

I entered the lift and turning the handle started its ascent. Before reaching the third floor, I attempted to straighten my clothes and discovered, much to my surprise, that I had mislaid my tie. I began to retrace my steps of the day in order to recall the moment when my tie took off on its own, but I found my mind strangled constantly by obscene images of Antonella, and so had to abandon the mental search.

The lift doors opened and I stepped out into a long corridor, along which were a number of doors behind any of which could be my father. I considered abandoning the visit altogether, but then I noticed a woman with a hare-lip standing in a darkened corner, smoking a cigarette from a long, bone holder. Her hair was bobbed and she was wearing a rather pretty flapper dress cut just above the knee, complimented by a pink feather boa. I estimated her to be about seventy or eighty years old, but I couldn't be sure. Women can be so clever about their age.

As I approached her, thinking to ask her the direction, she reached out suddenly and took my hand, and I noticed the red discs of rouge on her wrinkled cheeks, and the pitiful attempt to hide the deformed lip by camouflaging it with the Cupid's bow once favoured by an It Girl whom my father quietly admired in the 'twenties. Clara Bow, I believe, was the girl. An actress.

'I saw this blind man waiting to cross the road and so I offered to help him,' I heard the old woman saying, her voice trembling. 'I went up to him and said, "I'll help you across the road" because that's how I am. I'm very kind. But halfway across, halfway across the road, he suddenly—this blind man—he suddenly put his hand on my breast. You can understand how horrified I was. A woman of my demeanour being treated like a common ... I can't say the word. I just can't. I want to be sick at the thought of it. And then this man, this blind man, started to gibber at me. He said, "I'm sorry. I'm so sorry. I'm fifty-three years old and I've never touched a woman in all my life. I have no friends and I don't believe in God, so what is the point of living?" That's what he said and also that he hadn't been waiting to cross the road at all. He had been waiting for a lot of cars to come along so that he could walk in front of them. I'm thinking of reporting him to the police. A dangerous man like that, putting his hand on my breast. What kind of gratitude is that?'

I backed away from her, pulling away my hand, and she jabbed at me with the cigarette holder. I hurried down the corridor and then stopped and looked back at the sound of a crash. The old woman, attempting to follow me, had walked into an unseen wheelchair and had fallen to the floor. I watched her grope helplessly about the carpet, moaning for help, and I realized suddenly that, like the wretch in her story, she too was blind. I turned away immediately, and I wondered who painted the circles of rouge so neatly and so carefully on each of her cheeks, and who it was who pressed her dress.

*   *   *

My father was in bed and in the dark when I entered the room. He was in bed, lying on his side, staring out through the shuttered window at the strips of darkening sky outside. There was no one else in the room, big as it was, and almost no furniture except for a marble-topped table supporting a water jug and bowl, two chairs sitting knee to knee in a corner, and a dark mahogany wardrobe the size of a tank and equally as menacing. Heavy brass handles, fashioned into the faces of beasts, hung on the cupboard and on the doors and on the inside of the wooden shutters, and the heads of lions dominated the posts of the bed.

On one wall, opposite the window, was a print of El Greco's 'Toledo' in two colours, white and sepia, and on the adjoining wall a rather insipid water-colour of the Nile (three dhows out of perspective in the foreground, a pyramid and a sunset in the back) hung under cracked glass just over the washstand. There was no clock.

I closed the door behind me, convinced that he was dead and gone, and walked to one of the chairs in the corner and sat down. My father's eyes were staring fixedly at me out of a gaunt, lined face, and I found it hard to believe, not only that this was a man who was barely forty years old, but also that he was my father. To me, it was my first sight of a corpse, though instead of feeling chilled and nervous as I expected, I remember I felt remarkably relaxed and rather curious. Everything about the body (though only the head and one arm was visible) demonstrated its death, from the alabaster skin to the fingers of the right hand curled round the final unread pages of an Ambrose Bierce anthology, and resembling more the dried leaves of a palm frond I remember seeing in somebody's front room. Even when the eyes in the face blinked and I realized the bed's occupant was still alive, I could not accept this trance, this gaping stupor, as being a living thing. My father was dead—as dead as he was ten years before, and the only difference was that now the coffin was being varnished, and the limbs had almost stopped functioning.

I moved my head back into the gloom of the corner and became aware of the smell of age and velvet curtains. Outside, I could hear the blurred chatter of the evening promenade, as dry-eyed widows paraded their new hats, and young girls in starched dresses lingered too near the water's edge. The room itself grew darker, almost by the minute, until the pictures round the room were blacked out and all that remained of the wardrobe was the vague gleam of a brass eye and the hollow reflection of the white water jug in the long mirror. All the time I was aware of the eyes on the bed, staring at me, studying me, and once their owner actually stirred, and I heard the slow crescendo of paper on silk as a book slid off the quilted eiderdown, and dropped stealthily to the carpeted floor.

Perhaps, I thought, I ought to make the first move, and offer a 'Hallo' or a 'How are you?', but the moment had gone ten seconds after I entered the room, and I was no more capable of such a gesture than the man in the bed was. We were stalemated by our own pride, humility or whatever you wish to call it, and there was nothing I wanted more, just then, than to be a thousand miles away, on whatever compass point, with my self-respect intact. It was an impossible dream, but a small comfort.

I suddenly felt a cold draught on my right cheek as if the door had been opened, and somebody had entered. I could sense the man (for some reason, there was no question of it being a woman) standing just behind my line of vision, one hand still on the door-handle no doubt, and the other probably resting against the carved arch of the door. He must have stood there for at least a minute, saying not a word, and staring intently at my profile and the man in the bed.

For some reason, I was reminded of that dubious anecdote concerning Charles the First of England on the eve of his execution. Apparently, Charles spent his last night in St James's Palace, surrounded only by his wife and the young princes, hugging them to him as the final hours passed by, and telling them stories by the fireside to keep the children from crying. Only once were they disturbed, and that was just before sunrise when a man, wrapped in a cloak and hidden by a hood, entered quietly and stood in the flickering shadows of the room, head bowed. Only the low growl of the dogs lolling by the fire betrayed the stranger's presence, and even this was soon silenced by a word from the king. Finally, the anonymous visitor turned, opened the door and left the room, but not without a final, sad glance towards Charles. It was not until much later, when the king had been to the block and was dead, that the identity of the night stranger was revealed to be none other than Charles's own murderer, Oliver Cromwell.

It was this rather precious and yet disturbing story which came to my mind then, though it wasn't till years later that I realized how horrifying and how bitterly ironic the image was. I was then only aware that a stranger was there, and when finally I gathered enough courage to turn my head a little to the right and gaze at the man, it was too late. The door had been closed again and I was alone in the room once more with that dying man in the bed. The only indication that someone had indeed entered, and left, was a small spiral of orange peel lying just by the threshold of the door.

'I was bored with *this* life. What made the priests think I wanted one that was eternal?'

I lean forward, my hand in his, and press my ear against his mouth. The lips are cold and wet and I can hear the sucking of air in his lungs, and the frightened shudder of diseased flesh. I try to turn my head away, but my neck is held tight in his left hand and I gasp for breath.

'She wanted it all,' he is saying. 'She wanted the Blood, and the angels and the happiness and the heaven. She wanted all that. She tortured her mind for Him, and put herself on the rack in order to achieve a place in His heart. She loved Him, you know. I could never understand the emotion. It was too grand. Too big. It was too grand for me. Frightened me ... She loved Him because she believed He was good, and because she believed He was kind. I know that. She gave Him everything she had, even more than she gave me. She gave Him everything, and when she was happy, because I wanted her to be happy, she thanked Him. She thanked *Him*. She never got down on her knees for me ever. Not that I ever wanted her to, but ... For Him. She loved me too, I know. She told me and so I believed her. But she *adored* Him. Adored. If only I could have been ... And so He took her away from me before we'd hardly begun. She gave Him everything He wanted, and so He took her away. All she gave *me* was you. You. When she died, I went mad. If I hadn't, I would have killed myself. And so I went mad. You do understand, don't you? It was the only thing I could do ... '

I say nothing and listen to the faint murmur of his heart, far away in the distance.

'Do you know why I wanted you here?'

'Because you're dying,' I reply, my voice strained and broken.

'No. Because I want you to do something for me.'

54

'If I can, I'll try … '

He doesn't reply for a long time. I think again that he is dead, but feel his eyelashes flicker against my temple, and I shiver. My cheek is suddenly wet, and I fear he has coughed up blood or vomited base matter, and in one movement I wrench myself away and stare into his face. His eyes are sickeningly moist, and I see the tears glistening in the gloom.

'What?' I whisper. 'What do you want?'

As if on a hinge, his head lolls suddenly away from me and I follow his gaze towards the window.

'Can you hear me?' I ask. 'Tell me what you want.'

I am becoming impatient with this beggar. Why did he never write to me? Not even once. The man is mad. Of that, there is no doubt. I can smell his madness. Look at the grubby collar of his pyjamas, and that cracked handkerchief thrust vainly under the pillow. And what are all these books scattered on the eiderdown? The bed is covered with them. More books than space. What's this one? *Der Steppenwolf* by Hermann Hesse. It must be trash. Violent filth. And this one. *Demian*. By whom? My God, by Hesse too. Who is this Hesse? A madman, no doubt. A moonatic. *Siddhartha* by Hermann — are they *all* by him? How many did the grub write? No, this I recognize. This, I know. Kleist. Kl-eist … The man shot himself. Madness. Am I to be conceived by this creature in the bed? Is my birth in nine months' time to be the result of this yellowing carcass under me? Here, in a hotel of cripples and the spiders of Bedlam? God! God — why did I deny you on that rock? Why was I so weak that I sinned, lusted after that splinter? When this man finally dies, I will confess it all. Confess that flesh-act. Beg absolution. For I am truly sorry. My mind is racked, *racked* with penitence and my fingers scratch at the door. I kneel,

genuflect, scatter myself before you. God, please, please—
let me be your footstool.

I see, before me, my father opening his mouth to speak.

'What is it?' I repeat, stroking his hair, my lips brushing
the gallery of his ear with a kiss.

'You are your mother,' I hear him say. 'You are not
me. You are her. I have never wanted anything from you.
Not even your recognition. I, myself … I myself therefore—I want you to do something for me now. For the
first time. And the … '

'What?'

'I—'

'What?'

'Could you—'

'What?'

'Pray for me. I am afraid.'

I recoil, my hand scattering books, my lungs buckling,
and stand horrified in the centre of the room. There is no
more sound.

'Pray for me … ' he gibbers once more. 'Forgive me.'

All light has gone. Darkness. I can no longer see the
bed, nor the man in it, though I know he still lives. My
own body is split apart and my soul, black as pitch,
shudders in its bowels. I can hear my father's voice begging
me and I lean forward an inch, because I love him, but the
request is still the same. I want to die too. If this is too
much for you to endure, then bear with me. He will be
dead within the minute. Set your watch. And after that,
I will try and make you smile.

'Pray for me,' I hear, scything through my mind.

'I cannot … ' I reply, 'because I am unworthy of God's
love. I have sinned.'

'Pray.'

'No.'

I cry out in agony, cursing my own skin for rendering me helpless. Within the past hour. A mere hour ... The corpse's eyes widen and pierce the night, and I turn away in shame. I hear him sob.

'Do not let me enter the darkness alone. Pray for me ... I am just nothing. Please ... pray ... '

I hear my father choking his tears on the pillow and he cries out in despair, his fingers tearing the sheet. Outside, a boat passes before the hotel carrying two men and two women. Perhaps they are honeymooners touring the coast. Or one of the men might be a guide, and the other man is accompanied by his sisters. Then again, perhaps they are merely lovers. Italian, one would think. The dog in the stern is a labrador.

'No,' I reply once more, 'I am a sinner.'

But the words do not reach him. They dissolve in the air.

'He's gone. The wretch has gone,' a voice says behind me, and I find the room is filled with the inmates of the hotel. A stunted line of deformed women, staring abjectly at the bed. There are no tears (except, of course, from me), but the passing is probably regretted.

I seek out the owner of the voice in the gloom, and find the man from the beach leaning idly against a wall, smiling at me. He is chewing at a segment of orange. I am aware that he is evil, and I lower my eyes, but not for long. They are drawn towards him once more, and I find his right arm round Antonella's waist, and his left hand easing a moist slice of the orange into her mouth. A rivulet of juice descends her chin and is caught by her tongue, darting out like a bird from a nest to retrieve a worm.

A hag without a nose places two coins on my father's eyes, and a plover's egg in the gaping mouth. I kneel and kiss his dead hand, and hug his shoulder.

'Shall I run your bath, sir?' the man behind me asks, touching my arm. 'Or shall I run your shaving mug?'

The room is empty now except for the carcass and this stranger standing over me.

'Who are you?' I utter, peering into his face.

'Catesby?' he replies, straightening the collar of my shirt. 'Dam-ned Catesby?'

4

'When she died, she left him all her money. She was very rich. Now that he's dead, you are.'

'I was told it could be about a million pounds.'

'Oh, easily a million. One way or the other. Don't you think the driver is taking the speedometer too much for granted?'

'Speed is very deceptive—'

'Such a platitude.'

'If I remember correctly, we will see Verona after the next bend.'

'Shall I read out a poem I've just written on my knee? Shall I?

> 'Your hair is so sweet,
> So blonde and so neat—'

'Perhaps it wasn't Verona after all. Perhaps it was Padua. *The Two Gentlemen of Padua?* No, it must have been—'

'He hasn't said a word since we left Trieste. Not a word. I said you haven't said a word … '

'He's in mourning. He's in the black. Grief-stricken. He's in mourning. Mourning. Aren't you, sir?'

*   *   *

In those first few bitter weeks after my father's death, I was never alone. I suddenly seemed to be surrounded by a horde of nodding, grimacing faces who assumed classic poses behind my back, and whispered in low voices about things unheard. Wherever I went (and I must have visited a hundred towns) I could always be sure that if I turned and looked behind me, there would be a frieze of figures standing on a shore-line, or within the broken echo of a temple, talking amongst themselves, and now and again casting a sidelong glance in my direction. Who they were, and why they were there, I never discovered, though I was reassured that they meant no harm.

I remember that they seemed unusually tall and thin, and that their bodies were bent and disjointed, like marionettes, and that their necks were unnaturally long. Sometimes, they reminded me of a flock of carrion birds clustered around a fallen animal, but that perhaps is too vicious an image, for I do believe they had my best interests at heart. Once, in Hydra I think it was, I saw three of them standing silently in a vineyard. Two of them were facing me and the third, who stood in the middle, had his back to me. I must admit I laughed out loud, since I was suddenly struck by the similarity of the group to that famous painting of the Three Graces. It's a traditional pose and has been adopted by many artists — Botticelli, I believe, incorporated it into his 'Primavera'. Anyway, the scene amused me, especially as they were men, not women, and were fully clothed.

Another time — ah, but I ramble on a bit. Let me just say that not once did any of them ever speak a word to me, nor even shake my hand. They only whimpered among themselves or touched each other's arm or face, and, except for collecting poppies (which seemed to delight them), never interfered with anybody else. At Serifos, they went away. I turned and they were gone, and I never saw them again. I asked Catesby about their whereabouts, but he merely shrugged and said he had never noticed them.

He was always by my side, of course. Catesby. I suppose he acted as a kind of guardian, although he insisted he was simply a valet, and that I should treat him like the dog he was. Naturally, he was joking.

After Serifos, we went to Paros, then Naxos, then southwest through the limpid Gulf of Lakonia, to Zaracynthus, where my mother was born and was now buried. I wanted to visit her grave, but Catesby thought it unwise, since the cemetery was on a hill, and it was rather hot. So we abandoned the idea (I must admit I was disappointed) and set sail north on my yacht for Venice. The flowers were thrown into the Adriatic.

Any idea of my returning to school in England had been cast aside, since I was now a rich man (though barely nineteen) and consequently was advised to live like one. 'The rich', Catesby remarked one evening at supper, 'should never be educated. It makes them aware of other things besides money. And that is always a pity.'

'That sounds rather facetious,' I replied, attempting to be flippant.

'Only if one knows the meaning of the word "facetious",' he replied.

One thing that disturbed me about Catesby in those early days was his slight antipathy to my beliefs. It soon became noticeable that he disliked, even resented, my visits to the church, and even once or twice voiced an opinion against it. Of course, I shrugged it aside, and took it as mere ignorance on his part, though I couldn't help worrying about this rift in our relationship. I was not to know then how tragic that rift was to become.

Oh, I must tell you one anecdote relating to Catesby's anti-religious fervour, which I think is amusing. Remember, I did promise to try and make you smile. Well, it was my habit every morning to dress and go on deck before the sun had fully risen, and then to kneel and pray. The custom is very traditional, and I rather enjoyed the moment of peace in the early day, when I could be alone with God. At first, Catesby would snigger at this routine, or make sly remarks. But when I appeared to take no notice, he planned a more dramatic attack, which at the time was rather painful. One morning, as usual, I pulled on my clothes, which Catesby had set out for me the night before, and hurried on deck. I then walked to the bow of the boat and knelt down, only to discover an excruciating pain in both my knees. The agony and the shock were so intense, I couldn't refrain from screaming, and so brought two members of the crew to my assistance. It wasn't long before the source of the pain was discovered. Two drawing pins had been neatly sewn into the knees of the trousers.

That night, I cooked my own supper.

*　　　*　　　*

'A child of four goes to sleep in a meadow, and wakes up to find a battle is taking place around him. At first, he is frightened, but an elderly soldier, seeing the child (a boy), comforts him and carries him to the safety of a near-by copse. The child now is thrilled by the spectacle before him, and laughs in glee on seeing the horses and the scarlet uniforms and the roar of cannon. In no time, the old soldier is showing the small boy all the many interesting things to be seen on a battlefield, pointing out each shell and corpse with an expertise learnt only through long experience.'

I am lying on deck, face down, naked except for bathing trunks. We are passing Dubrovnik and my stomach is full. Catesby continues the story as he sets down a tall glass of beer beside my right thigh.

'The child is fascinated, oblivious of the death around him and the screams of men. "This is a rifle," the old soldier would say, "and that is the broken hilt of a sword. This is a cannon-ball, and that is the leg of a horse. And that is a helmet. And this is a pistol. And that is a dead body. And that—" "No, it isn't," interrupts the child, peering at the corpse of a woman. "That's not a dead body. That's Mummy." '

I turn over to allow the sun to tan the front of me, and upset the beer. The glass rolls along the deck, spewing out the liquid, and then comes to rest by the chipped nose of a head of Hermes I had bought near Athens.

'I'll fetch you another,' Catesby whispers in my ear, and I feel his hand lightly touch my leg. Then he turns and hurries down into the galley.

I ought to sleep.

* * *

When we approached Venice, it was late July. I have never really cared for the city, though I am well aware I am one of the few. It has always struck me as being the most unromantic city in Italy, mainly because it tries so hard to be the opposite. All those peripheral reflections and baroque bridges merely chill me, and I feel a synthetic shudder in my back and through my stomach at the mere mention of a gondola or a pigeoned piazza. I could never make a woman love me in Venice, but I could easily commit suicide there. I actually did it somewhere else, but that's by the way. Venice is a sad eunuch of a city, not even worthy of one of my more slender amourettes. Canaletto, I fear, must have been a cold, cold man at heart.

So, too, on reflection, was I at the time. Religion is

63

rarely served at room temperature, and all those incessant visits to draughty churches had played havoc with my emotions. Since leaving Zordar, I had attempted a violent purge of all sensual feelings, no matter how small, in a fervent bid to re-establish myself in God's favour. I had fasted, prayed and meditated, with all the passion I was capable of, and even contemplated the smug world of the monastery for a time. Recollecting my behaviour from this vantage point, it is difficult for me (and if not me, who else?) to appreciate fully the sick state of my mind then. A mere child, barely a virgin, tortured by the eyeless conceits of priest and monk, and rendered almost insane by the night-eyed guilt of my own sin. I was ready to enslave my body in a cloistered cell, cowering on the floor, for fear of God's denial. My soul had been black-mailed by the inhuman prelate, and I, believing myself responsible for my father's damnation, was even seeking my own. And all for a mere orgasm. God—do you realize the monster they are creating in your image? And, worse, did you realize the monster you were creating in mine?

Albinoni is a pretty village, full of butterflies and singing birds, and loose-tongued dogs asleep on high parapets. We stopped there just before Venice, and if you have the time, I would like to digress and tell you of an incident that occurred there.

On arriving at the town, I immediately sought out the church as usual, and spent an hour there alone with my beads, in a further effort to bridge the perilous gap between me and salvation. When I finally stepped out of the church into the sunlight, I found to my surprise that Catesby was waiting for me.

'I thought we'd take a little walk, sir. It's quite a delicate village, and might please you.'

I remember I smiled warmly at him for the first time since we had met, and clutched his arm.

'That's very considerate of you, Catesby. It does look rather pretty.'

'We could stretch our legs, sir,' he replied, leading me away from the church. 'Walk in the meadows and stretch our legs.'

'Yes,' I said. 'Yes, we could. Stretch our legs. On the boat, we can't.'

'No, sir. Not on the boat.'

And then he peered at me and added, 'You have spit on your forehead, sir. Spit. I'll wipe it off with this rag I have in my hand.'

'No, Catesby, that isn't spit,' I replied quickly, moving his arm away, 'that's holy water. From the font. I have it on the fingers of my right hand, too. See?'

I raised my right hand up before me, palm out, to show him, and he seized my wrist and stared at the fingers.

'But they're dry, sir. There's no water there.'

And then he held my hand before my eyes and leant close to me, his mouth against my ear and I heard his voice, low and hoarse, whisper to me:

'Question: If God created you in his own image, who do *I* take after?'

And then he laughed and sprang away, stepping backwards on the dry sand of the road, and stopped about ten yards from me. For a brief second, a flash of sunlight glinted on the heavy ring on his left hand, then he laughed once more and said:

'Let us go to the meadows, then, sir. I hear they are knee high in butterflies.'

*   *   *

'It was Christ's own fault that Thomas doubted,' Catesby said suddenly. 'He should have worn his reincarnation in his buttonhole.'

We had been walking now for half an hour, through long grass, and now up on the slope of a hill overlooking the village. If I looked back I could see the yacht in the small harbour below me, and then the tiny huddle of red-tiled houses clustered around the church. It was a lazy day; a day for collecting blackberries, or for appreciating *Alice*, lying alone in deep grass. It was still and hazy and sprinkled with the rustle of field-mice in the corn, and the distant drone of a bee. Catesby was climbing ahead of me, his legs wading through the scattered flocks of poppies, turning only to throw out another remark (he had been discussing religion) in my direction. I hurried towards him, slightly out of breath, and sat down against an elm.

'It's too nice a day to walk, Catesby. I just want to sit here and stare at the sky,' I said hopefully, stretching out on the ground and resting my head on the most comfortable portion of the tree.

There was no answer at first, and I assumed Catesby had gone on ahead, until I heard the guttural scratch of match on matchbox, and I turned to see that he was standing right behind me, and was lighting a cigar. I turned away again and tried to concentrate my attention on a butterfly (*Vanessa atalanta*) that had settled near my left shoe.

'Your father is not in hell,' Catesby said quietly, after a a long pause.

'I'd rather not talk about it,' I replied.

'He's not in heaven either,' Catesby continued regardless. 'Nor in purgatory, nor in limbo. Nor even in dear old Abraham's bosom. Wherever that is.'

I didn't reply, not wishing to join in the conversation.

I knew he was anxious to involve me in an argument, but I was not in the vein. Besides, his heresy was becoming irritating now and more vicious by the hour, and I refused to pander to it.

'Do you know where he is? Your father?'

Catesby was now squatting beside me.

'Please, let's change the subject.'

'He's in a box. That's where he is. And the only way he'll get out, is when he's sifted through it.'

'I think you're wrong, Catesby. I don't want to discuss it, but I think you're wrong. I was with him when he died. He asked for God.'

Catesby smiled.

'It's much easier for a dying atheist to seek God,' he replied, 'than for a dying Christian to deny Him.'

Below me, I could see a dog walking up the hill-path, sniffing at the grass verge. I stood up and brushed down my trousers.

'I think we ought to get back. I'm getting hungry.'

'Oh—are the forty days up already?'

'Damn you!' I shout and turn away.

Slowly, I made my way back down the hill towards the village. Fortunately, Catesby was silent throughout the journey, and at one point produced a bar of Cadbury's Milk Chocolate from his pocket, and offered it to me. I was delighted, and I must confess the delight was more at his kindness than the gift itself. The chocolate, by the way, was a little sticky and the top two squares were no longer there, but otherwise it was delicious.

'Thank you, Catesby,' I said.

'Not at all,' he replied, wiping my fingers with his handkerchief. 'I just wanted to show you how sorry I was for being so impertinent up there. Talking about your dead father like that.'

'Oh, that's all right,' I blurt out, embarrassed by his behaviour.

'No, it isn't, sir. It was out of place, and in very bad taste. Will you forgive me, sir?'

'Of course I ... I mean, you mustn't think ... that I am against—'

'Beat me if you wish, sir. I am a dog. A sick creature. I am gravel under your feet.'

I am broken with confusion and embarrassment as I see this man debasing himself before me, and I throw my arms vainly in the air to push him aside. I loathe myself for causing him this humility and cry out:

'Catesby, it is all my fault. I shouldn't have snapped at you. It's just that—'

'My shoe-lace is undone.'

I spin round, and in my confusion find my hands grovelling through the grass and touching his shoe and I fumble for the laces. Above me, I feel him staring down at me, and I look up. I can see his eyes piercing mine and in them I can see nothing but loathing. My skin goes cold, and I realize that this man, this valet, this master, hates me. At this moment in time I am aware not only that he could kill me, I am also aware (and my breath rattles in its cage) that one day I will kill him.

The laces are tied and I rise and wander towards a low ridge on the hill and gaze down at a quiet field of flowers. A young girl, no more than five years old, is sitting in the middle. Her hair is the colour of a halo, and her face is as gentle as that of a young swan. In her hands is a daisy chain. As I look at her, I am reminded of Antonella. Dear, sweet Antonella.

That night, when I undressed, I was pleasantly surprised to see on my jacket the faintest imprint of the young girl's heart.

*   *   *

The next day I ate well.

Wheaten flummery, followed by a dish of lampreys (seven little holes behind each eye. Count them.). Sule-bubbles and a stew of pigeons. Tansy or *jaune mange* to follow, depending on taste. I myself prefer *jaune mange*, but the oranges must be from Seville. Claret, shrub, and have you tried *noyau* lately?

'Tomorrow, we will be in Venice,' Catesby remarked as I was about to retire. 'I have never liked Venice, sir. It's a eunuch of a city. I could never make a woman love me there, though I could easily commit suicide.'

'If that is so,' I replied, 'Canaletto must have been a cold, cold man at heart.'

'On the contrary,' snapped Catesby, 'I think his painting of Eton is superb.'

Not wanting to continue with such a trivial subject, I walked away, stopping only to say:

'Anyway, I've decided to skip Venice altogether and go straight to Verona. We'll buy a car.'

5

The town is behind me now. Behind and below. I am sitting on the highest step of the arena, and before me I can see nothing but cobalt sky and white marble. My horizon once belonged to the Roman matron and the senator's mistress, and to the peddlar from Antioch passing through the town with jars of spice. Around me and against me, elbows jostling, sandals split by rough stone, sit the matinée mob, clamouring under the hot sun over the death of a Samnite. The tiers, seats, stalls are packed now with a blurr of white and purple, and down there on that pathetically small oval of sand some animals from Tuscany and a larger one from Carthage are politely entertaining the crowd. Constantine visited here, and so did Dante. And so did Machiavelli, pausing under an arch, forefinger against cheek. And so too did Romeo, chattering on the steps with Capulet at heel. For this is Verona, at last, and I am in it.

I remember russet stone and cobbled alleys, and baroque acne on the faces of the clocks. The suggestion of silks and harlequined tights, and medieval cooks labouring over Roosted Connies.

'That sounds terribly fey,' commented Catesby, reading over my shoulder one afternoon.

'They're only diary notes,' I replied, my hand edging towards the page. 'Anyway, they're private and not to be read until they're published.'

'Is that a fact?'

'Well, *if* they're published. I—'

'And what about this drivel? "With a moist eye to the future, I hope love is exactly how the poets described it. I'd hate to find out that it was slicked up to fit the pentameter." Is that supposed to be witty? I don't think it's witty. Is it supposed to be?'

'Give me that back. Those are private.'

'I think it sounds puerile. It tears very easily too. You're not Oscar Wilde, you know.'

'Would you give me those damn pages back! You've no—'

'Actually, Oscar Wilde was dumb, but his chimney sweep was a neat ventriloquist.'

The wastebasket is emptied once more, and Catesby draws the curtains and pours the brandy.

'What are you writing now?' he asks quietly, settling down into my favourite chair, slippered feet resting in the hearth.

'I'm describing the arena. In Verona.'

'Ah yes. The arena.'

It is quite empty, of course. Not yet in ruins, though, like a tooth, it is decaying out of sight. The sand is tidy, newly raked, and there are obvious indications that once the arena could actually be flooded for a mock lake-battle, or for one of those erotic tapestries Nero seemed so partial to. You must have read about them in your youth, when the orgies of the past seemed more accessible than the orgies of the present.

One of them I recall (I think it was Nero, but it could have been Tiberius. Or even dear old Claudius. Roman emperors are awfully repetitive at times) consisted of a rather naive, but presumably potent young man, usually a Greek, strapped to a rock. The rock was in a lake, and the lake was in an arena, just like this. As the wretch lay on his back (naked of course), a secret door opened in the rock beside him, and three beautiful women appeared, also naked, but with their gorgeous pelts dyed various colours. Blue, green, yellow and so forth. The women then proceeded to release the youth and make love to him in full view of everyone, and presumably with some enthusiasm on both parts. I would have thought it was quite a pretty picture, especially with the colours and the reflections in the water. It was also, I hear, rather horrifying. For as the women and their lover were cavorting on the rock, they were unaware that a second door had opened and that half a dozen hungry lions were now making their way towards them. The grand finale of this spectacle (twice during triumphs and once on Imperial birthdays) was the eating of the four naked lovers by the lions, followed by a somewhat tired water-ballet performed by a group of patrician toddlers.

All this, alas, no more. Apparently a miracle play is produced here now and again, and once a year there is a local rendering of *Romeo and Juliet* (what else?), but no more lions, and certainly no more rainbow nudes shuddering out their last orgasm for the price of a ticket.

The names are still there, etched on the corners of the seats, and around the bleached pillars. GAIUS. OCTAVIUS. LIVIA. JULIA. VESPASIA. The female names chipped hard and strong, as if by an impassioned lover, long-since dead.

Numbers too. We can count them together, as we climb the steep steps to the top. Count them out loud. Come on, we are quite alone. XIV, XV, XVI, XVII, XVIII ...

I am sitting at the highest point, my back resting on the rim of the arena. Above me is a jet, a rare sight, flying diagonally across the sky. I watch it through shaded eyes until it disappears into the distance. On my lap is a copy of Milton, a poet I have been trying to appreciate since Hydra. So far, his talent has bypassed me.

> When the grey-hooded Even
> Like a sad votarist in palmer's weed,
> Rose from the hindmost wheels of Phoebus' wain.

The temper deceives me.

From this height, the genius of Roman architecture is breathtaking, and the legendary acoustics rather unnerving. Already, I can hear a voice clearly (of a man) and he hasn't even appeared on the sand below me. He is still in the tunnel. Listening more intently, I can almost make out each word, though not speaking Italian I cannot understand them. Yes, I can. I could have sworn I heard English words. Listen. Did you hear it? The man said 'rainbow', quite clearly and quite distinctly. And he hasn't even appeared yet. Probably some English tourist, knotted hanky on his head, with his myopic wife.

Ah, at last they come into view through the main gate below. I see them, a man and a girl, walking on to the white sand, and pausing, slightly stunned by it all, before the empty seats. The shadows are long.

Unobserved, I feel like a spy and study their movements as if they were under glass. It is too far to see their faces clearly, but by their attitude to each other, I can work out something about their character. An amusing game. They are obviously very close to each other, and may even be lovers. Yes, I would go so far as to say that they have at least made love. She touches his hand and his arm easily, without pre-thought, and yet still remains in her own entity. Ah, the man is lighting a cigarette, and doesn't even offer one to the girl. But not through meanness or lack of consideration, but obviously because he knows the girl doesn't smoke. Especially in public. I am surprised

73

they are silent, but probably the arena is something to contemplate without discussion.

The man is now walking across the sand towards one of the aisles. He walks with confidence, though not rigidly and self-consciously like a soldier or a priest. There is total control over his body, almost an arrogant control, and yet he walks lightly, hardly disturbing the sand. I would go so far as to say that he barely leaves any footprints.

The girl is following him now, though not hurriedly, like a slave, but taking her own time. He is certainly the stronger of the two, but she has a mind of her own. She has chosen to be the weaker with this man, but I feel she could have chosen to be the reverse, if she desired.

As to their physical make-up, they are still too far away to describe accurately, though the aisle they are approaching is the aisle directly below me. The man is English (why doesn't he speak a bit more?) but does not in any way resemble the average Englishman abroad. Unless that Englishman abroad is Lord Byron. Yes, that is rather an apt comparison. There *is* something Byronic about the man, something aristocratic and slightly decadent. Perhaps it is the haughty angle of the head, or the cut of the clothes. Even his attitude to his mistress (this type of man would never be seen in public with his wife) reminds one of the hero of those Regency novels where fashionable bucks only talked to women over their left shoulder. The girl herself obviously adores him, and I would even guess that they have just made love. Within the last half-hour, she was under him. Perhaps, though that is seeing too much into things. I am not a magician, nor wish to be. Ah — the man is looking up and I can see his face quite clearly now. Yes, the features are quite distinct. It is Catesby.

The book falls from my lap and I stare in amazement

74

as he makes his way towards me. This is no idle tour. Catesby has deliberately sought me out. I gawp, stunned. Not only is his arrival unexpected (he had mentioned something about fishing), but his appearance with a girl is a revelation.

I watch him as he climbs the stone tiers. He doesn't look up, but keeps his eyes levelled at the steps above him. Finally, he stands before me, a little out of breath and looks down.

'Fine day,' he remarks.

I nod and he sits beside me. I become aware of the girl and turn towards her. She is quite pretty behind dark glasses, and her blonde hair is cut short to her head. Her mouth is a little familiar.

'Don't you think she looks prettier now?' I hear Catesby say, and I see the girl sit on the step below me and remove her glasses. It has only been four months at the most and yet she looks two years older. My body suddenly collapses and I cling on to the stone step. Next to me, Catesby leans forward and puts his hand on Antonella's shoulder and gently massages her neck. I hear her moan.

'She's pregnant, sir,' he says casually, and gives me a brief smile. 'And what we'd both like to know is, what are you going to do about it?'

Antonella has also, I gather, developed a penchant for parsley.

6

'I must apologize, Father, for being held up but you have an awfully rude— Oh, I'm so sorry. Shall I begin? You must allow me a moment to collect my thoughts ... You see, I don't speak Italian. Latin yes, but Italian ... Well, it's been one, two, three—five days, *five* days since my last confession. And since then—you want me to go through with it?—yes. It's been five years, *days*—I'm so confused. I cannot see ... One moment.

'Now. Since then I have told lies. Told—lies, Father. Missed mass, missed confession, missed communion, missed— It's a very pretty church this. The nave is especially delightful. Did you design the altar cloth yourself? If I could just get down to what I wanted to say. You won't believe this, Father, but I'm being spied on. There's a man. I won't mention his name but it's Catesby. Catesby. With a C. And he is trying to worm his way into my confidence. Of course I won't have it. I've told him. "I won't have it," I've said. It started off as just a passing acquaintance. Just a How Do You Do. He wanted a job as my valet. Well, he was smartly dressed—oh he was, Father. I noticed it, but do you know—it didn't stop there. He had evil designs on my person. I noticed him spying on me, turning my friends against me. This man. But I couldn't stop him. This sounds very childish and looked at objectively, it is. It is. But I can't escape him. I feel linked to him. He gave me this suit. I told you that, didn't I? This suit. Look at it. I mean, I can't be seen in public dressed like this. But I'm trying to give it up. All this way of living. Oh, yes.

'I'm thinking of settling down somewhere on my own. A nice little beach hut perhaps. On the coast. Somewhere near the equator. Lying on the sand with the sun, with the sun, with the sun beating down on me, and watching the sea and the waves beneath my feet and all the little nignogs splashing in the surf and singing songs. I'm thinking of that. But I've got to get away. It's imperative that I move. A man of my position. You can understand that, Father. With all your ... worldly ways. If I stay here much longer, I think it will drive me—

'I have to be on my own. It's the only way of being sure of myself. Of being with God. Of not—being deceived. When I was a boy, when I was young, a child, when I was eighteen I encountered a woman of social standing who had a delicate face and delicate eyes and a quiet manner. She wasn't a pretty woman, though many thought she was, but I didn't somehow. I'm a man of the world you know. I've been around. I've seen ... Anyway, I never thought of her, this woman, as pretty and so fell in love with her, and thought of her and lay awake at night dreaming of her, recapturing movements, gestures, questions, undertones, meanings, smiles. She became an irritation to my logical self and I took to leaving my soup before supper, until I abandoned it altogether and began immediately with the main course, and then abandoned that too, discarded, filled up the evenings by walking with her, side by side, in the woods near Ravenna talking about Dante, and other such local talk, and visiting old temples and collecting bits of Imperial Rome together like coins and vases and ears from statues. Riding. Then when I was nineteen, we met face to face for the first time, and I learnt her name, Father. It was—it was—Antonella.

77

'Well, we got on rather well, and I found she shared my interests, and not only that, she shared my distastes too and hated Dante like myself and thought that Ancient Rome was a terrible bore what with all that in-blood and everything. So of course we got on famously. I think that's the expression. I met her father. You would have liked him. He's dead now, of course. Died suddenly halfway through reading *Anna Karenina*. Tragic really. He would have liked the way the story turned out. Her mother was already dead like mine. She's dead too. Well, anyway, we decided to get married. Well, *I* decided and she agreed, and we fixed the date and I got everything ready being the bride's father—I mean the bride's groom—*bridegroom* —and I ordered the cake and arranged everything down to the last crumb.

'And on the day of the wedding, as I was standing at the altar, a tragic thing happened to me. I was standing there. At the altar. With Antonella on my left, and the best man, the best man on my right. Then all of a sudden, all of a sudden, the best man leaned towards me and whispered in my ear, said to me—he said—I can't say it, Father. Of course, I realize I am merely teasing you, because you don't understand a word I say. Do you? Ay? Not a syllable. Are you deaf? DEAF? Oh, God, it's all lies. Lies. If only you knew. Lies. All—I'm only nineteen. A mere boy. A puppy. Pup. A mere—*stripling*. She lay there and I had to, and now, well ... Look at me. Father, look at me. Through the grille. Look at me. I'm going mad, aren't I? Am I? Or are we *all*? ... I wish there was a light in here. I've become afraid of the dark. Spiders. Antonella's hand ... Oh, I think I ought to leave. I'm really wasting your time, Father. When I get going, I can empty a hall.

'I don't like it in here. Cold church. Talking too much.

Why *can't* you smoke in a place like this? Just because God — Oh, I'm being blasphemous and I wouldn't be insulted if you threw me out. Well, at least I tried a confession about … But seriously, I feel better after evacuating my bowels than after evacuating my soul. Thank you, anyway, Father. I'll find my own way out. Father. Father? Oh — he's gone. Gone. I am alone again. As usual … '

*   *   *

'Have you made up your mind, sir?'
  'Yes.'

*   *   *

I can see her in the garden. She is wearing a yellow dress. Her head is turned away from me and she walks across the lawn towards a row of lupins. Somebody out of sight, out of mind, makes her laugh and she throws her hand before her mouth in that enchanting mannerism of hers, and blushes slightly. I open the window and she looks up, but she doesn't wave.

I can hear them making love in the next room. Silence. I lie in bed clutching a crucifix to my ribs, and listen to the night insects on the terrace outside. A sudden moan, a depression of sheets, a shattered crescendo of sighs. A scream. An orgasm. A condensation of a shudder. Silence. Each night, my ear to the wall, listening to Antonella whimpering. Each morning, Catesby brings me my breakfast. Orange juice, coffee and croissants.

I realized in Verona I could never get her back, no matter how hard I tried. She was infatuated by him. *Him*. Whatever had gone wrong was irrevocable. She allowed me to touch her stomach, of course, to feel the child inside her. But that was all. A hand, face down on her stomach, tip of fingers nestling in hair, and an expectant pulse from within the womb. That was all I was allowed. Not even a kiss. From that moment on, we could only become friends, discussing platitudes in public and never meeting in private. Between a love affair and a friendship, friendship is far the more tragic. It lasts longer.

On the coast near Rimini, a few miles east of Lomva, there is an orchard. It is perched high up on the cliffs, and stretches from a low valley up to the foothills, and then stops abruptly above the edge of the sea. In parts of it, sheep wander, and they do say that one section of it is so dense, it is impossible to see the sky through the leaves. Vergil probably wrote about such an orchard, and if he didn't, he ought to have done. It is a place for composing sonnets or for creating myths. Daphne was chased through those trees and Narcissus died here. Catesby and Antonella took me there one morning, and I vow I will never go near the filthy place again.

She walked on ahead of us, stopping only to pick up a fallen apple or to point out a squirrel. We would both nod and Catesby would shout out an ecstatic cry of congratulation, then put his arm round my shoulders and whisper confidingly:

'She's just a child, you know. Really. That's all she is. Just a ... child.'

After half an hour, Antonella was about two hundred yards ahead of us, and once or twice she was even out of sight. Neither Catesby nor I hurried after her, and I knew it was because he wanted to talk to me. I took my time, and discussed irrelevancies such as the weather or the English sense of humour. Finally, he stopped altogether, and proceeded to preoccupy himself with the branches of a tree. I waited.

'You've been very good about this, sir. I must say,' he said at last.

I pretended innocence.

'How do you mean?'

'Well ... ' He broke off a twig. 'I'm sure you are aware that she and I are ... '

'What?'

'You're not that naive, sir. She's a little whore and we both know it. I at present am the one who's on top of it. That's all.'

'I wouldn't touch her.'

'Of course not.'

'She's not worth—'

'No.'

'She makes me vomit.'

'Profusely. Ha! Well, I'm glad that's cleared up. I thought perhaps there might still be—'

'No. Nothing.'

'I'm so glad, sir. I did wonder. First love and all that. She did mention that you were a little pathetic to say the least, but one can't have everything, can one?'

I see Antonella reappear in a clearing ahead. She is watching me. She stands in profile and I see the gentle swelling under her dress where my child lies in darkness. I would give anything for it not to be mine, but it is. I know it. Of that, there is no doubt. And that is all I need to say.

'She's very expert for her age, sir. Very surprising. No holds ba— How old did she tell you she was?'

'I never asked.'

'No. Well, she is in fact sixteen. Comes from a Lombardy family. Mother's English. Or was. Dead as a doornail now.'

Sweet Antonella. Am I really in love with you? I see the soft down on your arms caught in the sunlight, and your hair cut close to the head now. What magical drawer or box or casket contains those sheared, discarded locks now? One day, when we are alone, you must show me. Oh, Antonella—why am I tortured by you, torn apart? I am aware of you hovering in the mists of cornfields. Or standing alone by the edge of a pond, butterfly net in hand. You are frowning over a spot discovered on your chin, or merely avoiding my gaze. Sometimes, often, you are just out of sight. Perhaps Catesby is right. Perhaps you loathe me. But even that emotion excites me, because it is yours. In your innocence, you are unaware of the sacrifices I will perform on your altar.

Catesby touches my elbow.

'Let us join her. Come on.'

We approach and she stops between a thought, and drops a browning apple-core to the ground. Catesby draws her to him, arm round her thin waist.

'They say this clearing is pagan. That covens gather here on Sabbatical nights, and the sky is scorched with ritual.'

Antonella giggles and looks around. I, too, notice that the trees form a circle, and the ground is sloped as if in an amphitheatre or hippodrome.

'What happens?' she asks breathlessly, and I watch her eyes widen.

'They have a mass,' replies Catesby, one hand caressing her rounding stomach. 'A kind of mass.'

'With a priest?'

'With a priest. Though not a collared prelate. This priest appears in the shape of a goat, with horns and a disguised face.'

'Why a goat?'

'Because of the horns and the cloven feet.'

82

'And what does he celebrate?' she asks.

'The devil. Beelzebub. Old Nick.'

'And what does he use as a chalice?'

'A chalice.'

'And what does he use as wine?'

'Blood.'

'And what does he use as an altar?'

'The naked body of a girl.'

'Dead?'

'Alive.'

Catesby and Antonella have begun to sway, as if in a trance. Side to side, gently to and fro.

'And where does the naked girl lie?'

'On the ground.'

'Face up?'

'Face up. Legs apart. Breasts the gospel, thighs the epistle.'

'And the priest?'

'Ah, the priest ... '

'Will you — ?'

'Be the priest?'

'Yes.'

'If you will be the altar.'

'All right. If *he* will be the blood.'

They turn towards me, and Catesby reaches out his hand. I back away. Antonella laughs and pulls the dress over her head. For a moment, she is held with it, caught under her chin, her thin body contorted, then the dress is released and drops to the ground. She stands in the clearing in her underclothes, and Catesby slides his hand slowly down her back and under the thin cotton of her pants and brings them down to her knees. Her stomach, round as a ball, is exposed to me. I notice deep scratches over her breasts.

'Four more months and it will be as flat as when you once laid on it, sir. Her tummy ... '

Antonella laughs and suddenly pulls up the pants, scoops up her dress and says blithely:

'I think I'll go back to the house. I am hungry for parsley. Goodbye.'

I watch her as she walks away, through the trees.

'What a whore,' Catesby whispers with a snigger. 'What a little—'

'You bastard,' I reply like a fool.

'Oh yes. I know.' He laughs, then takes my arm.

'About the baby, sir. About Antonella. Have you made up your mind yet? Remember, the bachelor who spurns his illegitimate children should take great care he doesn't marry a sterile wife. So, tell me your mind, sir?'

'Yes,' I answer.

Catesby frowns and moves aside, pensively. Then turns back towards me, his eyebrows raised.

'And?'

7

Now that I am dead and gone and in my coffin (and a cheap one at that—it's leaking already), I find myself debating on my decision regarding Antonella. Of course, nineteen years have gone by, and when I finally quit the earth to lie underneath it, I was a far wiser man than I was then. And yet I still believe I did the right thing during that hot, oppressive summer. What my true motives were are vague to me, but it *was* the right thing, and of that I am sure. By 'right thing', I mean right to Antonella and her only, and not to anybody else. For, let me say, that if you are one of those cabbages who dictates his behaviour according to those twin farts, Social Etiquette and Social Fashion, then I trust you will have a good day, and will replace this book immediately where you found it. For I loathe and despise you, and shudder at your foul company. I have seen you expose your bigoted, cowardly, grubby soul in a hundred cities, in a hundred countries.

It is you who is the parasite of trend, ordering his life and the lives of others according to the shiftless, shallow moods of the day, whether they be in art or morals. It is you who erected the gallows, and pointed the finger and trod on the night hide of your neighbour. It is you who dares to cast the first stone again and again and again, and I despise you because you are sick, a maggot in my flesh, and I vomit at the thought that I am crucifying myself before someone like you. But then, this is not a tract, nor meant to be, and so I will not continue with my abuse. It was unwise of me to begin, and I regret it. A little. But I shall let it stay. The point has been made, and what follows is simply beside it.

Of course the Child is father to the Man. But not *every* child, and not to *every* man. *I* was then, in that fatal year, and when Catesby took my arm in the orchard and asked me for my mind, I told him my decision wisely, even though it turned out to be one of the most brutal I ever made. All my life, I have been constantly surprised how fragile women really are. They are frail creatures, easily broken, no matter how they may appear to the untrained eye. Naturally, they try to be strong, to be independent, in order to disguise the crystal of their souls; and so you must treat them as if they were strong, control them, rein them like a horse. But you must never forget the brittleness underneath. It is too easy to break a woman's heart. Any fool with a profile can do that. That is no achievement. That is just a rather selfish and immature pastime designed for the ignorant. I exploited that frailty a hundred times and more, in those grubby, vile years of my last decade, and always with success. I do not boast about it. I merely confess it. I even, earlier on, made many women love me, for the sake of it, and that too can soon be learnt, if such venom is your trade. But the hell was in those final years, when I could never make a woman *like* me. Not even for an hour. That, *that*, is the agony. Some women I have known or heard of have gone insane and sought the preci-pice, because they loved a man they despised. The very — but I digress too much, too soon. It is not time yet for me to pull down my trousers and reveal my sores to you, even though you may be eager to peer and your sandwiches are almost eaten.

*   *   *

'I will marry her,' I replied, treading on a dead apple. 'If that is what she wants, I will marry her.'

That night, the servants walked heavily on the stairs, and fell asleep on the lawn. Antonella revealed a talent for the piano, and sang:

Fare thee well, my dear-est   dear, fare thee well

over and over, much to our delight. She had a sweet singing voice, rather high and light, and very endearing, and could also sing in French. I myself consumed two bottles of Burgundy, and threw one of them up amid the wisteria. Then, at about three o'clock in the morning, I went for a walk along the cliffs in order to clear my head, and Catesby went to bed with my future bride.

*   *   *

The girl was so still and so quiet that one would have thought she was either dead, or not a girl at all, but a waxwork dummy somebody had found and propped up on the swing. She was very pretty and young and was wearing a two-piece bathing costume. It was not a bikini, which was surprising, since she looked the kind of girl who would only wear bikinis, and not this high-waisted, boned creation favoured by European girls until the early 'fifties, and by American girls (always the prude), until the early 'sixties. One would assume then that the bikini was not yet in vogue, and that this was perhaps just after the war. The girl's dark lipstick and hair style seems to add to this assertion.

She is sitting on the swing, her hands lightly clasping

the ropes, and is gazing down at the rows of Mediterranean villas below her. Her expression is more wistful
than sad, and on the grass beneath her feet lies an abandoned copy of *Forever Amber*, page-marked by a *Photoplay*
magazine. Next to both is a half-empty glass of orange
squash, complete with a chewed paper straw and a
drowned wasp. The girl, whoever she is, is also about four
to five months pregnant.

Ten yards away, behind a Riviera palm, a young man
watches her anxiously, staring at the back of her neck, as if
debating whether to talk to her or not. His face is slightly
flushed, and now and again he glances nervously to his
right and to his left, and then back towards a house
nestling in the trees at the end of the lawn. Finally, his
hand straying to the knot of his tie, the youth begins to
walk slowly towards the swing. His shadow reaches the
girl first, and her eyes flicker and she raises her head
slightly, aware of his presence for the first time. On the
ropes, her knuckles clench and turn white, then relax.

'Where's Catesby?' she asks, without turning her head.

The youth, startled, stops suddenly and doesn't reply.
The question is repeated and with more emphasis.

'*Where's* Catesby?'

'He's ... gone to the village,' comes the stammered
reply. 'To ... see about some wine.'

'Did he take the car?'

'Yes. He ... '

The youth now walks round the swing until he is in
front of the girl, and stands, left leg rigid, right leg bent,
looking awkwardly at the tranquil scene below. No further
words are exchanged, and the girl herself even closes her
eyes as if to banish the intruder from out of her sight as well
as out of her mind.

'Have you read this?' the boy asks, picking up the book.

'No, and now you've lost my place.'

'I'm sorry—'

'No, you're not. And now I'll never find my place again.'

'Oh yes, you will. Tell me where you were in the story and I'll—'

'No, it's a silly book. I don't want to read it.'

'Oh.'

The book is placed back on the grass, the magazine is placed on top, and the youth, red-faced, stands up once more.

'I thought perhaps you might like to go for a walk?' he asks hopefully.

No answer. The girl flicks a fly from her bare shoulder, and starts to sing to herself.

'It's quite nice farther along the coast,' the boy continues. 'Caves ... and places like that. Tunnels. You might like to see it ... if it won't tire you.'

'Don't like caves.'

'Well, they're not only caves ... We could walk down to the sand. You haven't—'

'I might fall. I'm pregnant. You did it.'

The girl now sets the swing in motion, heels pushing against grass, and begins to sway back and forth higher and higher above the boy.

'I just thought you might be bored,' he calls to her, and she laughs and pulls a face.

The boy stands lost, bewildered, under the arc of the girl, eyes flicking back and forth, lower lip under top, then despairing turns away. Immediately, the swing jerks to a halt, and the girl slams her bare feet on to the ground, shuddering the tree above.

'Where are you going?' she demands.

'Swimming.'

'You can't go swimming. I want some more orange squash. This is warm. Get me some orange squash.'

The boy stops and looks at her, his cheeks red. A mere arm's length away, the girl places her open mouth against the taut rope of the swing and lightly bites it, her teeth sinking softly into the fibre. Then, moving her head slowly round it, she allows the rope to slide gently up and down between her lips until it is glistening and wet, and her tongue is darting along it, and into it, and over it. All the time, she studies the boy through half-closed eyes, now and again closing them altogether as if on the edge of dreaming.

'And a straw,' she says breathlessly. 'I must have a straw as well.'

The boy moves away, then, as if the very word was reverberating through each pore and muscle, he answers:

'No.'

The reaction is dynamic. A stifled gasp from the girl, an initial flicker of annoyance in the eyes, and then it is replaced (but only for a second) by a look of surprised admiration. The head then turns away, nose tilted, hair swivelling round the neck and the coldness returns, only slightly tempered.

'If you're nice to me, I'll let you kiss me.'

'Now—how do you mean? Nice?' he asks.

'Well, you know,' answers the girl with a slight yawn, 'empty the ashtrays and call me Diddums. Things like that.'

Below her, she sees a group of holidaymakers walking down the cliff path towards the beach, rolled towels under their arms. Two of the men among them wave, and a third shouts out a remark but it is lost in the air.

'Antonella—why do you treat me like this?' the boy blurts out, with astonishing melodrama. 'I mean, we're getting married next week.'

This, naturally, makes the girl laugh and the men below turn once more and wave. This time, Antonella waves back, and even stands up, her hand covering her stomach. She then becomes aware of the boy again.

'Stop staring at me.'

'Do you hate me, Antonella?'

'Look at my breasts. They hurt. They're getting heavier and heavier and they hurt. Catesby says they might start to sag and never go back to normal.'

'Antonella—'

'I'm beginning to get pains in my back too.'

Defeated, the boy slowly turns and walks away, not towards the beach but back up the lawn to the house.

'Where are you running off to now?' the girl shouts after him.

'To get your orange squash.'

'All right. But if you see Catesby, tell him I'm down here and that I want to go swimming.'

On the patio of the house, a man stubs out a cigar and moves back into the shadows.

*   *   *

' ... and then I've been thinking about your shirts, sir. When we get to London, we'll buy two dozen. That will do for a start, sir. From Turnbull and Asser, of course. That warm hound by the hearth. Oh—and talking about clothes, sir. I found this soiled silk handkerchief in Antonella's knicker basket. Fancy someone leaving a soiled silk handkerchief amongst all her dirty underwear. It *is* yours, isn't it, sir?'

*   *   *

Two days after the engagement party, I got drunk again. This time however it was on vodka mixed with Lemon Barley. I remember, I found it a pleasant drink, and in no time I had consumed three-quarters of a bottle, and was ready to finish it altogether, when I heard the shower go on inside the house. Above me, I could see Antonella's yellow swimsuit hanging over a window-sill to dry, and then I heard her voice singing faintly above the water.

I gulped down another glass and walked across the patio, tripping over a forgotten broom.

The bathroom door was open and I entered unseen and unheard. As I closed the door quietly, I could see her yellow bathrobe arranged over a chair, her Basque slippers lying on the stone floor, and my face, thin and drawn, in the bathroom mirror. The shower curtain (pretty little seahorses on a field of green) was almost closed, leaving a gap of three inches where I could see her, oblivious of me, soaking her body. I held my breath, hypnotized by glimpses of brown flesh—a nipple, a delicate hand smearing soap under an arm, inside a leg, across a shoulder. I watched water cascading in rivulets over that thin, young girl before me, and I stood paralysed, a worm of the worst order, wallowing in my own base thoughts. I loved her then, foolishly and ridiculously, and I wanted to kill her, to impale her like a butterfly on the study wall. To fashion her into a flower I could carry in my hand. I hated Catesby more than I could ever say, because she went to *his* bed at night, and I was left only with an agonizing prayer that lately hadn't even been acknowledged, either by God or by my dear, sweet Antonella.

The shower ceased abruptly, and she stepped through the curtains and stopped. There was no shocked cry of indignation, nor even a syllable of abuse. She merely walked past me as if I didn't exist, as I were a mere tile on the wall, and coolly took a warm towel from a cupboard in order to dry herself. I wanted to die. I couldn't even talk or move, or even breathe, because I was nothing. I didn't exist. I could only occupy some wretched space in the room as she rubbed the towel over her body and sprinkled talcum on to her drying skin. The creature even started to sing to herself, and once even sat on the toilet, but it was only to trim her toenails. My stomach heaved, and I could feel sweat gushing down my chest, trapped under the thick sweater.

Finally, she blew her nose on a paper tissue and wrapped the bathrobe around her, and left the room, and I only just made the bowl as I vomited out my heart.

That evening, Catesby returned from the village, and the three of us ate supper together on the terrace. The conversation was subdued, and I left half of the meal and abandoned the wine.

'You don't look well, sir,' Catesby said. 'Is it the fish?'

'No,' I replied.

'Perhaps it is wedding nerves. They do say the prospective groom goes through hell before the day. And often *after* it too, I gather.'

Antonella smiled.

'Have you thought about a honeymoon, sir?' Catesby continued.

'Well, I—'

'I myself would suggest Paris. Though I feel that in order to appreciate Paris completely, one should visit it only once in one's life—very early and very briefly, and then never again. Imagination and recollection will take over within a week, and within a mere month the magic will be complete. It is a sad city the second time, but the first adventure, especially on a honeymoon, could be enchanting. Don't you agree, Antonella? Yes, I think we ought to go to Paris.'

'So do I,' Antonella replied quietly, fashioning her napkin into a crown. She hadn't spoken a word to me all evening, or even glanced my way. Of course, I was but a child. I knew that. No woman wants to be reminded constantly of the weakness in a man, and that, alas, was all I could offer. Catesby only wanted her to lie by him when he snapped his fingers, and she adored him for it. I couldn't even fire him, tell him to pack up and go (even if I had the strength), for Antonella would leave too, and I would never see her again, no matter how hard I tried.

That night I dreamt differently. My sleep was usually plagued by quiet visions of Antonella floating downstream, surrounded by minnows that darted in and out of her, or of her lying naked in a manger of soot whilst my finger wiped her skin clean, centimetre by centimetre; or sometimes of her standing in a quarry wearing a halo around her head as if it were a new hat, and with eyeless sockets from which butterflies peeped out. You see how erotic my mind was becoming. Abstinence, whether voluntary or forced, encourages masochism, and often leads one to perversion or to the brink. It is the frigid wife who makes the husband the adulterer, and the Puritan who produces the deviate. But I myself was harmless. Sexual fantasies, of course, but so far I hadn't lingered my hand on a child's chubby leg, or followed the whore under the arch. I merely tortured myself with images of my bride-to-be over and over again, until I woke up sweating to the sound of her moans in the next room. This night, however, I dreamt differently.

I dreamt I was sitting in a church. I was just sitting in

a church facing a statue of Saint Sebastian. It was carved out of wood and stood in a small chapel, barely lit, and the face was the face of Catesby. A statue of Saint Sebastian with Catesby's face, and with the arrows stuck in the naked body. Here and here and ... I just sat there and looked at the statue, at the face, and at the arrows, when all of a sudden blood began to trickle from the wounds. I thought, in my dream, that perhaps it was my eyes. That I was tired and I was seeing things. But then I got up from the bench and walked over to the statue and touched the legs of Saint Sebastian. And then the arms. And then finally I put my finger on the base of the arrows just as they entered the wooden flesh. It was wet. Red. On the end of my finger. And then I licked my finger, and it wasn't blood at all. It was all my imagination. It was wine.

That was the dream.

*　　*　　*

I am to be married tomorrow. A quiet affair. I am not nervous about it, nor am I, of course, blasé. I am just sick with fear.

I had been ill for the past week, and had spent most of the time lying in bed or on a canvas bunk on the terrace. A doctor had been called but never arrived and so I was left in the hands of Catesby, who served me cordials, and sometimes dry biscuits as a special treat. I never saw Antonella once during that mild convalescence, except when I caught a glimpse of her through the bars of the balcony as she sat in the garden, or played with a kitten she had bought from a local farmer.

On the Monday, my health improved sufficiently for us to leave the villa, and drive north-west into France. I was

95

placed in the back seat of the car, wrapped in a tartan blanket, whilst Antonella sat in the front. If I raised my head slightly and moved it a little to the left, I could smell the shampoo in her hair.

Catesby drove fast and rarely stopped. Hardly any words were exchanged between any of us except casual comments about the passing landscape or the state of the road. Now and then, I would attempt to open a discussion on some topical subject, and once, in a rare good mood, just outside Avignon, I even suggested a word game we could play to pass the time. However, the idea created little interest and so was abandoned.

Then, on the eve of the wedding, we arrived, late in the afternoon, at Brioge, a small village, and decided to spend the night in an auberge there.

Antonella went straight to her room and locked the door, and I decided to spend my last day as a bachelor bringing my diary up to date.

At eight o'clock, just as the light was fading, Catesby knocked on my door.

'I thought it might be a good idea, sir, if we both went for a drink. I understand that it is customary for the men to celebrate something or other on the nuptial eve. What do *you* think, sir?'

I closed the book and placed my pen back in the drawer and nodded.

'All right, Catesby. I think I could do with some fresh air.'

I could also do with some company, since I am never happy alone. He smiled back at me, hesitated at the door and then said:

'I'll meet you downstairs, sir. Near the desk.' And then left, only to return immediately, hand raised in emphasis, to add:

'May I offer my congratulations, sir. About your future

wife. I'm sure many men will envy you. Many men ... '

We walked for about an hour, through the dark lanes and then across empty fields punctuated only by a forlorn scarecrow or a small group of cows. Catesby drank continually from a hip-flask (a mixture of Cognac and Benedictine) and told endless jokes, mostly violently obscene, about honeymoon couples and wedding nights. He was in a good mood and obviously trying to be considerate, so I relaxed sufficiently to join in the laughter, fortified by a full bottle of wine.

'Oh, and let me tell you about Hopkins,' Catesby mused, anticipating another anecdote by a short burst of laughter and another swig from the flask. 'Odd man, Hopkins. You would have loved him. A chemist, I believe. I was introduced to him in Nicosia, when he was serving with the British Army there. Poor old Hopkins. Had to marry a Cypriot girl whom he mistook for a taxi-whore. But I must say he was admirable in his unselfish devotion to his wife, despite that. I remember that even when she was just the slightest bit ill, he would summon the vet immediately.'

I laughed out loud at this, and almost fell into a ditch. My unsteadiness was greeted by loud cries of 'Woops!' and 'Upsadaisy!' from Catesby, and then he drew back his arm and threw the flask high into the air. We both stood and watched it soar through the night sky, its metal case glinting in the moonlight, and then it fell about twenty feet away, disappearing behind a hedge.

'Let us find a bar, sir,' Catesby breathed into my ear, clutching my arm. 'A tavern. The night is still young and tomorrow ... Ah, tomorrow ... '

There was only one bar in the town, surprisingly. It was called Les Gémeaux, I believe. I remember that in half an hour both of us had six plastic coasters stacked up on the marble-topped table before us.

'It's incredible how identical our tastes are, sir. Isn't it? I mean we both drink exactly the same brandy. The only difference is that you pay for it.'

'And we both like exactly the same woman,' I blurted out through an alcoholic haze. 'The only difference is that I will be married to it.'

A brief smile touched Catesby's mouth and then he lit a cigar and stared idly into space, not saying a word for a long time. Finally, he exhaled a deep cloud of smoke and said quietly:

'I read in a book the other day that it is rather dangerous to make love to a woman after she is five months pregnant. I'm not sure whether that is strictly true, but it was there. You can't make love, unless of course it is from the rear. It was there. In this book. Did you know that?'

'And Antonella is—'

'Oh, five months easily. Perhaps five and a half now. Mmmmm ... Pity about that, sir. Especially on your honeymo—'

'But you have been having it every minute of the night,' I shouted angrily. 'You knew that. *You* knew it.'

Slowly, Catesby stubbed out the cigar and turned towards me, his face emotionless, and stared innocently into my face, eyebrows raised.

'I have been *what*, sir?'

I blushed crimson and looked away. Strange how alcohol is so unreliable. It so often lets you down just when you most need it. I stammered a vague reply, I don't know what, made an excuse to go to the toilet and left quickly, knocking over a glass. When I returned Catesby had gone.

*

I found him standing outside the inn where we were staying, telling further jokes with the concierge. When he saw me approaching, he turned his back and laughed even louder at a remark I couldn't hear.

'Catesby!' I shouted, gesturing to him to approach. I had consumed a further bottle of the local wine in his absence, and was determined to make use of its deceit before it was too late. Catesby raised his head slightly in my direction, looking at me as if I was a scab, then sauntered arrogantly towards me, flicking imaginary dust from his sleeve.

'Sir?' he asked, staring casually at the dark banks of trees around the town.

'Where have you been?' I shouted, red-faced. 'I've been looking for you everywhere.'

'Ah, but unlike God, I am not everywhere.'

'Is that supposed to be funny?'

'Funny? Blasphemous perhaps, but hardly funny. I never laughed. Did *you* laugh? The concierge certainly didn't laugh. Hardly funny. On the other hand, if you wish me, sir, to say—'

'I don't wish you to say anything any more. After the wedding tomorrow, I want you to leave. I'll pay you an advance then you can go on your way. I don't need you any more.'

I began to tremble. Catesby, on the other hand, made no reaction whatsoever.

'Did you hear what I said?' I continued.

'Of course. Don't you think it's a lovely night? Not too hot.'

'Damn you!' I shouted and hurried away.

Catesby immediately sprang after me and grabbed my arm, pulling me towards him.

'You cannot damn me, sir, because I don't believe in

hell. Nor in heaven either, come to that. On the other hand, one day perhaps, I will damn you. If need be.'

And then he released me and wandered back into the garden without looking back.

*   *   *

That night was a strange night. The temperature had risen decisively, and by midnight it had become unbearable. The heat weighed oppressively over everything, and I soon found I had to strip the bed of every covering including the sheet, and even then the sweat began. Of course, I couldn't sleep. There was no question of that. I could only lie and stare at the ceiling, or attempt to read. My head was throbbing, mostly through the wine, and the whole atmosphere of the room, the night, the bed, took on a macabre quality. I remember I wrote a paragraph about it in a notebook, but that has long since disappeared.

At about one in the morning, when the inn was finally silent and the only sounds came from the trees, I decided to take a walk in order to clear my head of the wine, and perhaps calm my nerves. The scene with Catesby had disturbed me, I must admit, though I couldn't rationalize why it also frightened me. But it did. In an odd way, I regretted the argument and even contemplated an apology, a retraction, washing of hands. I was well aware that it had been sparked off because of my insane jealousy of Catesby, and I was prepared to tolerate it for that. Jealousy is a common enough disease, though I would never consider it a healthy one. It corrupts the mind, warps it away from the truth, and the truth was that I myself was pitifully weak, worthy of nobody's love, neither God's nor Antonella's, and least of all my own.

I wrapped a silk dressing-gown around me, found slippers for my feet and wandered out first on to the balcony outside my window. It was a little cooler under the night sky, and there was even a slight breeze. Below me, the whole village was asleep, except for some wretched mongrel, abandoned without any supper. I noticed then that the balcony itself ran along the whole front of the inn, and so realized suddenly, my skin tightening, that it must at some point pass Antonella's room. I immediately dismissed any thought of proving such an assertion, but then drawn out of curiosity I decided to take a slow walk, just in case, on the pretext that it was only an innocent stroll. And so I lit a cigarette, casually flicking the match into the garden, and began to amble along the balcony towards the corner. I passed three windows, curtains drawn, and stoically refrained from glancing in. Because of the heat, they were all open, and once I heard snores.

At the corner of the building, my promenade was stopped by a railing, and so, reluctantly, I turned to retrace my steps, and abandon any thought of voyeurism. However, as I moved round, I discovered that the window directly on my right was lit by a table lamp or a wall light from the room behind. The curtains were also drawn back. I stopped, holding my breath, and silently slid close to the edge of the glass. There was no sound from within except for a strained breathy staccato as if someone was in pain. However, from this angle I could see almost nothing except the dim glow of a light and the gold frame of a mirror. I realized I would have to be even more ambitious, and move into the centre of the window itself, and perhaps even move my head right into the room. I was now reckless.

Quietly, I edged along the balcony, almost upsetting a potted plant some fool had placed in the darkness, and found myself staring directly into the room. The picture I saw was all too clear and I found I had to dig my nails into my flesh to stop myself screaming. They were in there, both of them. Standing there, in the centre of the carpet, hunched over, and she had to cling to the brass rail of the bedstead to support herself, and to support him, while he … Oh God, why do you have to punish me like this? I recoiled away from the window, my body shivering like a dog, and jammed my fist into my mouth to press down the vomit. I turn, and turn, and then my scream hits the air, and I try to run. Catesby grabs me before I have covered a mere yard and spins me round. He stands there, naked, staring into my eyes, hypnotizing me, and I hear his voice murmur:

'Didn't you know it is unlucky to see the bride before the wedding?'

And then he is laughing and I am dragged into the bowel of the room where she stands, wild-eyed, and in my hand is the base of a lamp and I am bringing it down on her body and on her back and on her stomach over and over again as her screams sear the air, and then it is all blackness and night and the worms of the dark. Oblivion. I am a dead thing.

*　　　*　　　*

I awake to the sound of rain spattering through the leaves outside my window and I am in my own bed. It is morning.

And now I am in the church (fifteenth century with renovations) and standing before the altar, my head bowed. I have chosen the dark-blue three-piece suit since it is a special occasion, and wear a carnation in my buttonhole. In my mind, I go over the correct procedure for the bridegroom, and I must say, without boasting, that

I am almost free of wedding nerves. It is a happy day and I find it hard to repress my smiles as I hear the organ playing above me and the anxious coughs and nose-blowing from the host of guests sitting in the wooden pews behind my back.

She looks adorable of course in white. It is definitely her colour, and I make a mental note to buy at least half a dozen dresses in that colour for cocktail parties and other such affairs. On my right, Catesby stands stiffly to attention, and I swear he is nervously fingering the gold ring. For once, I feel superior to him, and I smile once more. There are no butterflies in *my* stomach, no sir. Not even a caterpillar.

Naturally there is a hitch. There always is at weddings, isn't there? It's all part of the ceremony. A slight delay, an anxious moment. This time, the priest seems to be late in delivering the classic question. I am not surprised at this, since he has probably never seen such a handsome couple as I and my beloved Antonella. I straighten my back proudly, and in order to allow the priest to relax I gaze around the pulpit and look up at the crucifix and the leaded windows and above that at the sky. The sky? Water is trickling down my face and my clothes are soaked by the rain and I turn round in horror. I am, of course, alone.

The church is a ruin, crumbling under Napoleon and bombed within the last decade. There are no pews, no organ and no priest. There is not even an Antonella. There is only me, in my best suit, standing in the mud before the shell of the altar, crying out 'I will! I will!' to the blackened walls and the gaping windows.

No one hears me, not even God. And then as the rain pours down over me, I begin to sing a hymn I have remembered since childhood.

Part Two

REALITY

Snatch the fig-leaf from the nude if you wish.
But do not be surprised if it reveals—a fig.

Catesby

8

As an atheist, I have never fully appreciated that absurd ritual of submerging the human body in a few gallons of water. It is an attraction that apparently fascinates millions, and yet, so far, has left me utterly cold. I myself wouldn't have got off my donkey even to glimpse John the Baptist, let alone join the queue, though, let me say, I do think Salome was a little harsh, to say the least. Old John obviously knew his audience, and was well aware that most men seem to equate the cleansing of the body with the cleansing of the mind, and always will. As a baby, I was prepared to submit to my baptism with only the minimum of noise, and if during that rather wet and nasty process some spiritual grace seeped into my soul, then I will accept it as a rather dubious bonus. But no more. You will not catch me tethering the cow and jumping into the Ganges, nor will you find me standing behind you, wrapped in a sheet, as you wait for the municipal bath at Baden-Baden. I don't give a fig for fat Neptune and all his properties, and if he tries to push his medicated trident into *my* bathroom, I will summon the police immediately. No, the popular myth of baptism is not for me. I don't believe it does anything but open the pores and introduce you politely to pneumonia.

I remember visiting that bathing pool the Church of Rome has in Lourdes and being appalled at the thousands of pilgrims anxious to dive into water that had only been used to wash the sores of the sick. These same people would not dream of sharing their tea-cup with the coloured maid, and yet crossed continents in order to wallow in the waters of the dying. To me, the only miracle was that they managed to get home to the kids in one piece.

Let's face it — if one is to go along with this fanciful belief that water cleanses the soul as well as the body, then surely one should choose the finest water that has been brushed only by the beautiful bodies of young girls, newly talcumed and newly scented, and one should surround the water with sweet-smelling flowers and shaded palms. The Church of Rome hasn't got such a place, but the Church of Hollywood has several. One of them belongs to the Beverly Hills Hotel which is where I am now, lying on a green settee under a yellow canopy, surrounded by the priests and acolytes of the order, as they smoke their cigars and talk long distance to their temples in New York. Beside me is a tall red-headed girl (a model, no doubt, but not a Vestal Virgin, thank God), who lies asleep within her scarlet bikini, and allows my hand to cruise her bare back and the forehead of her bottom, my fingers dipped in Ambre Solaire. I can hear the incessant demands of the telephone operator as she summons the faithful to the shrines in the corner where they listen at black phones, nodding obediently to the clamours of the hierarchy, and snapping their fingers at the dickied youth by the bar trolley. My own glass is refilled constantly as I lie like a slug under the brilliant blue sky, shaded from the head, and gaze at the bouncing breasts and lowered eyes of actress and whore who pose on the diving board, blonde hair framing dark glasses, or linger near the oldest and the fattest, laughing over-loudly at jokes they don't understand. The water is blue, the palm trees are plentiful, the bourbon is iced, and the senses are delightfully teased. An unholy of unholies without a doubt, a celluloid heaven, but who can resist it? Just for the day? Certainly not I, as I approach my thirty-eighth birthday. Certainly not I.

Faces turn towards me, hands are raised in summary recognition from across the pool, and sunglasses are lowered by manicured fingers as curious eyes study me from under false eyelashes. The girl beside me stirs in her sleep, turns over on to her back and opens one eye to reassure herself that I am still there. She then gives a half-smile, reaches out for her glass of Coke, finds it empty and falls back to sleep again. I don't blame her. She had a hard night.

I gaze at her face as it lies in profile. It is indeed beautiful and I think once again (but I know in vain) that she is the one I seek. Her eyes (closed now, yes, but open— ah ...) are large and round and are the eyes one has seen in a dozen paintings of seventeenth-century courtesans, honeyed-sepia, enigmatic and adorable. Peter Lely painted them until it became an obsession, and women at the court of Charles the Second would have given their right arm and their title to possess such eyes, even for a day. Strangely, I noticed her mouth first when we were introduced. Perhaps because in her mouth I saw something familiar, something ... Her nose is man-made. This she has told me. It's a fine nose and probably an improvement on the design of God, who, if the paintings of the Virgin Mary are any indication, has rather a bourgeois taste in women.

'Are you hungry?' I murmur.

The girl doesn't answer. Her mind is full of dreams. I wonder what they are, what kind of visions flitter through that head. Of me, perhaps. Of last night? Ah, no, a slight frown has touched her forehead. That cancels me out. Dreams of me are invariably accompanied by a smile and a low sigh. I say this, not out of conceit (though I am not short of that), but out of experience. I cannot recall the number of times I have watched the faces of women at dawn as they snoozed beside me. The expression is always the same—placid, dimpled and utterly contented. Once I asked one of the women what she had just dreamt and received the reply: 'Babies.' Same thing. Women who love their lover invariably dream of babies with supreme optimism. Men, on the other hand, only dream of babies when they loathe their lover, and then with fearful pessimism. This girl here (her name is Harriette) no doubt dreams of babies.

I would of course be a fine catch. Handsome (somewhat), experienced, rich, and quite famous around the boudoirs of the world. Housewives in Manchester have heard of me, and so have their gym-slipped daughters. My infamy as a playboy has even reached Paris, that smug, snobbish little capital, and I have been told that scandalous tales, all no doubt absolutely true, are being circulated at this very moment in Seattle. I have become a universal stud, the subject of endless dirty jokes, but I take it all in my stride. Men hate me because they believe I am nothing but an unprincipled lecher with altogether no respect for property. This is probably true, but I know they secretly envy me because they foolishly think I am a superior lover who performs miracles between the sheets. About that I will refrain to comment, but I can say that prowess as a lover has nothing whatsoever to do with physical qualities. Only the oaf in the gym believes that. No, the art of sex (if it has to be put in this intellectual nutshell) is based on the phrase: relaxation of the body, preoccupation of the mind. Just that and nothing else. Follow that, and a man can enchant a woman in bed for hours on end until she is delirious, and never once will he spoil it by his own orgasm. Unless of course he wants to, but

I always find that the male orgasm is an awfully time-consuming impediment. It should be reserved for the end of the night, and not brought out as an hors d'œuvre. Anyway, I will not elaborate further, for why should I give away my secrets? Besides, it's all in the Koran, which is where I pinched it from initially, and then lent it, after much persuasion, to Aly Khan.

'Are you hungry?' I repeat to Harriette. She frowns again. I lean across and kiss her on the shoulder, and for a moment, a brief moment, she is lying on a rock on an island in the Adriatic many, many years ago. But it isn't her. I turn away. It isn't her.

I lie back and stare up at the sun. A few yards away I hear jazz being played on a transistor radio, and across the pool a girl laughs. I cannot see who it is, nor do I know the situation, but by the tone alone I know what the message is. It means: 'I know you want to sleep with me but you are hideous and a bore and I am only tolerating you because you might be useful, though you've got to offer me a bit more than dinner at Perino's and a posy in the mail.' Smart girl, myopic man. Young actresses rarely discover till it is too late, despite the precedents, that the most sought-after parts are their own private ones.

I finish another bourbon and signal for more. Lately, it has become more than a habit, and sometimes I find myself seeking out a night partner merely to distract me from my own thoughts. I never saw Antonella again after that tragic night many years ago, though I have looked for her ever since. I am aware she lost the baby and so realize how much she must hate me. For weeks I could never enter my own bed without thinking of hers, and how she was sharing it. It wasn't with me and it certainly wasn't, alas, with Plato. And yet ...

I think of Catesby too. He was gone when I returned to

the inn, though I am assured it was not with her. I try to believe that but the nightmares crawl over me. He was such a weak, pathetic creature, with his pitiful beliefs in God, and that poetic, masochistic view of women. Has he never learned?

'Are you hungry?' I murmur again and she shakes her head, and the mane of autumn hair curls round her. My eyes stray along her body (long torso, superb hips, legs not too good), and I feel very tender towards her, perhaps more towards her than for any woman I have known for a long time. Harriette. Yes, I shall remember you with fondness.

'Can I have another Coke?' she says, opening her eyes. I gesture to the waiter and point to my empty glass. The girl beside me lights a Parliament cigarette.

'Get in the shade,' I tell her. 'Your skin will peel.'

She looks at me but doesn't move.

'Do as I say,' I continue. 'Your skin is too sensitive for this heat. Besides, I have never cared for lobster.'

At first, she still doesn't move. You know I'm willing to accept that God created Man, but I'm convinced that Leopold von Sacher-Masoch had a say in the creation of Woman. Ah, she moves, shuffling her body over the tiles and then resting her arm on my knee.

'Shall we drive to Monterey after lunch?' she asks, slotting herself into my plans.

'I won't see you this afternoon,' I reply, looking anxiously for the waiter who seems to have disappeared. 'I'm going away for a few hours. I'll see you later this evening.'

'Oh,' she answers, disappointed, 'I see.'

But she doesn't. Of course she doesn't. How could she understand? I am lost in a labyrinth which I myself don't comprehend.

And yet she doesn't insist. I like her for that. It's a rare quality. Instead she stands up, gives me a brief smile and walks towards the water. Everybody watches her of course, especially the women, eyes narrowing, teeth grinding out a fox-trot. Then, with a splash, she is in the water and I am left alone with an empty glass. I think I will go to the beach this afternoon. On my own. I will go to the beach where the surf is. They say the girls accumulate there in droves. Rather like puffins.

*   *   *

There is an ancient Indian Song of Songs called 'Gita Govinda', which tells us in somewhat overblown terms all about the famous Hindu playboy, Krishna the shepherd, who apparently lingered near quite a few streams in his day, and watched innumerable naked milkmaids dabbling amid the bullrushes. The record of his conquests is enormous and though I don't care for his technique (dark-eyed moody overtures, reams of poetical natter, coupled with heavy sighing and threats of suicide. Very old hat), I must admit I admire the man's stamina. Especially for a farmer's boy. He apparently had absolutely no scruples whatsoever (a dying art), and would lay anything down, and if not on the grass, then under it. But even *he* didn't take his rug to California, and I don't blame him. There comes a limit to everything, and no seducer in his right mind would go there to pluck anything else but oranges. The very *hygiene* of the women is enough to send you back to Mummy.

There they are, on the beaches and in the soft-tops—the over-fed, over-scrubbed and totally sexless girls of California. I saw them everywhere that afternoon. I stood on the dunes and gazed at those breasts of America as they jostled over hearts of pure plastic, fearful to penetrate any one of those golden gates in case the orgasm they produced (if any) turned out to be soda water. And after the tenth creature had stomped past me, I prayed to God that Antonella would not be among such a gaggle. She wasn't.

After an hour, I retreated, and left them with their male counterpart as he flaunted his limp surfboard before him. It was a tragic moment. I have been told that people actually have sex in California, and that a certain brave doctor even documented some of it as proof, but I personally don't believe it. It's all a huge hoax. By God, it must be. Show me your shepherdesses, Krishna. Make room for me in your tent, and I will play you a dozen ragas in *thumree* style till even the sacred cows come home.

I drove back slowly to the hotel. It was still afternoon and still hot, but all thoughts of women had been trampled from my mind. I switched on the car radio but that didn't ease my detumescence, and so turned it off again. I was restless and depressed. The scenery offered no release — one doesn't look at scenery in the Gold Gate State, one merely drives through it — and the flask in the glove compartment was almost empty. Why did the image of Antonella persecute me so? Why did her face, eyes closed, hair fingered by the wind, drift before me wherever I turned? She was gone. She was not by my side, her head on my shoulder, telling me stories of her childhood and the seas of Arcady. She was gone. She was with someone else, perhaps married. My flesh tightens and I accelerate the car. Carl Jung talked of the *anima* within the man, the female that destroys the reason and leads him to the rocks. In the Orient they call her 'the poison damsel', and already I feel the venom staining my blood. Was Antonella my Lorelei, and if so, then show me the precipice before I live another second. The car now touches ninety miles an hour.

I suppose basically I despise women, though I must

114

immediately qualify that statement before you label me a misogynist or a latent homosexual, or any other of those pet phrases you are so eager to launch at the unknown. I have said many times that the man who attacks all women is probably only attacking one in particular. But do I attack Antonella? Forgive me if I toy with my thoughts. I never really loved the girl and often I called her a whore as I lay by her night after night, day after day. More often, I didn't even want to sleep with her, but did so in order to tease Catesby who lay in the next room clutching a crucifix to his chest. And yet Antonella plagues me. If only those grubs who follow me from capital to capital, laughing at my jokes and smelling my sheets, knew what kind of man they dealt with. Women adore me. There is no question of that—the speedometer is reading ninety-five—and I am well aware it is because I treat them with a warm arrogance they find hard to resist. When you finish the book, take off your glasses and look at your wife for the first time. The masochism is there, of course. You cannot ignore it. That need to be dominated no matter how weak is lying there. Dismiss it, and you will slowly lose her. Your daughter too.

Oh, I admit I generalize. But so often the hand on my pillow bears a wedding ring, and the stomach that cries for more carries the scars of birth. My dustbin is filled with housewives' billets-doux, and my telephone rings loudest during office hours. It is sad that many people marry out of loneliness, but it is tragic that more people get divorced because of it. Worse, the major catastrophe regarding frustrated old maids is that they are all married. Do I sermonize too much? Perhaps so. But the speedometer is touching a hundred now and there isn't much time. There never is.

No, I don't despise women. Some, of course; I am not

perfect. Why, I remember swearing at that female Cerberus attending the toilet in Bruges, and didn't I insult you when you were hostess of that dreadful Manhattan soirée last spring? If I didn't, I will this autumn. But women in general are adorably sad creatures who have cried on my shoulder so often that I may have to ask my tailor to cut my jackets accordingly. If I survive the wreck. One hundred and five, I see. The arrow is quivering and so is the car. Speed hasn't really appealed to me but this is rather enjoyable, though I do wish that motor-cyclist behind wouldn't make so much noise. Antonella ... I saw you once, you know. Within the last year. You touched my hand and whispered in my ear. But it was only the acid that splintered my time and sprinkled my mind on the ground like coloured confetti. It was a cheap escapism designed for fools, and so I will shun it.

My hands are off the wheel and the car is beginning to slide. I feel myself on the verge of ecstasy, and then suddenly I cry out. Where will I go? Catesby knows because he has paid his stamps, but I? I could not bear a void, which is all I envisaged, nor could I stand a devil, especially since I don't believe he exists. That would be too much of a sick joke. But I am saved at last, though not by God, nor even by Zeus. His name is Meyer and he is acquiring a paunch. I apologize profusely and he hands me a ticket, and then roars off towards Los Angeles and I follow like a snail, grateful at least that my breath smelt only of garlic.

When I reach the hotel, I got straight to the bar. It would be foolish to find Harriette (she is no doubt still by the pool) since I am not in a strong frame of mind and I need to drink alone. I am not, like many men I have met, averse to the company of women when one is fully dressed. I merely prefer to be alone more often than I choose to be with company. I order a large bourbon and retire to a booth in a corner. I am aware of two women looking at me and nod over-enthusiastically. They immediately glance away embarrassed and busy themselves with their gin. Tomorrow I will go to San Francisco, one of the few cities in America I like, and will relax with some friends there. I say friends, but they are mere acquaintances who tolerate me. I have no friends any more. They all left me when the apron strings began to strain.

After an hour, I have drunk almost a fifth of bourbon and feel decidedly better. I say goodbye to the barman (Henry) and return to my room and ask for Harriette to be paged. She is in my bed before the light has faded. Below, the pool is emptying and only a lone attendant wanders slowly round it collecting the towels and straightening the chairs. Near the diving board, he stops and lights a cigarette and stares wearily at the twilight.

'My parents have found out I am with you,' Harriette sighs, gazing abstractedly at the television screen.

'Oh?' I reply.

'They're very angry.'

'Parents always are. See if there is any orange juice in the fridge.'

She gets up and walks slowly to the door. She really has the most remarkable body and isn't that a divine beauty mark on her shoulder?

'They don't want me with you.'

'How did they find out?'

'Someone must have taken a photo of us when we were at Chasen's.'

'If there's no orange juice, bring me a glass of milk.'

On the television, there is the inevitable panel game. I stare at it blankly. She returns with a glass of beer. I take it with a resigned shrug.

'Have you ever heard of the Mann Act?' she asks, sitting beside me on the bed. I run my finger down her spine.

'Isn't that what we've just been doing?'

'No, the *Mann* Act. Two n's. It's a law forbidding you to transport a minor across a State line for purposes of fornication.'

'The beer's warm.'

'I forgot to put it in the ice-box. Anyway,' she scratches her nose, 'apparently you can be arrested and put in prison.'

'Oh really? Are *you* a minor?'

'I'm seventeen years old.'

'And that's a minor?'

'Yes.'

'The man who wrote that law must have been either blind or pitifully deprived.'

'Don't you care?'

'Only if it affects you.'

'I'll leave tomorrow.'

Why is this girl so kind, so selfless? She puts me to shame.

'No, *I'll* leave,' I reply.

'You don't have to.'

I find myself smiling and I kiss her on the cheek. But she doesn't respond. Why do some parents believe that they are the only ones who can make their children happy? This girl is worthy of a hundred parents and should never be sad. Instead she is being smothered. Perhaps I was lucky. I never even had a home.

'I know I don't have to, but I'm going away anyway tomorrow. On my own.'

'Where to?'

'New Orleans,' I lie.

'It's nice there.'
'So they say.'

She was asleep when I left. She was asleep and her red hair covered her eyes. She was asleep and lying on her stomach and her face was turned away from me, and I could only see the fingers of her right hand on the pillow before her and the back of her head. I would miss her greatly. That I knew. Perhaps I would see her again but the glance would be sidelong and the cheeks would be slightly flushed. No, it was over. It had to be. I am not a sadist nor want to be. I have never hit a woman, either physically or mentally. I haven't even done it if they have asked me to. And so I could not make her suffer any more. You weren't Antonella, Harriette. And if you are reading this now, think of me. I, on my part, remember you with a bitter pleasure. Bitter because I hurt you, and pleasure because you never hurt me.

I close the door and I lean against the foliaged wall-paper in the corridor. I suddenly realize that the leaving is not as easy as it was ten years ago. Five, even. Then I would walk out on a woman without a second thought. But now ... Is it age or is it weakness? I shiver. Damn the girl. Damn everything about her. Her loveliness makes me almost human.

In the car I snap at the chauffeur and complain miserably of the heat.

9

The bay itself teases me. I catch glimpses of it at the end of avenues as they duck out of my way, and sometimes it is even beneath the wheels of the trolley itself. One cannot escape it in San Francisco and no one in their right mind wants to. I stand on the platform of the Powell and Hyde as it lurches over impossible gradients and I feel excited for the first time in months. There is no girl clutching my hand, nor is there even a jar of whisky in my stomach. There is just the bay, and the sun and the quiet elegance of the town. California's roundlet.

I get off at Fisherman's Wharf and hurriedly take a long taxi-ride across the bridge to Sausalito. A village once inhabited by bosuns and the old men of the sea, talking of clipper ships and gazing in the early hours across the water at the hills and the Pacific beyond. They are all gone now, of course, and their houses now echo to jazz and esoteric discussions of poetry. But the ghosts are there, and it's a warm comfort. It stirs in your brain and you become a child. I remember volumes about a hundred cities. I remember names and statistics and histories and could write a guide without straying from my chair. But I remember almost nothing about San Francisco, and couldn't even tell you the date of the Fire. It doesn't matter. The town is in my eyes and that's all I can say. Another word and I will become positively mawkish. Yes, I'm glad I came here.

I walk for hours through the hills and down into the wharves and later I take the ferry, the *Harbor Queen* I believe it is called, and sit on the deck as it chugs slowly across the bay to Belvedere. I can see the dark forests fringing the water and at one point we pass the empty skull of Alcatraz. I begin to drink, unable to hold out much longer. I lean over the rail and stare at the water, not actually drinking the bourbon, but clutching it in my hand, secure that it is there. I still cannot refrain from glancing into the face of every blonde who passes by, in case she is ... And then it is dark and I return to my hotel. I am to be interviewed by one of those female avant-garde magazines I have never heard of, and with great reluctance I have agreed. I will of course select the photo they use to illustrate the article. One can never be too careful where one's image is concerned. Especially at my age.

*　　*　　*

Q: May we begin by asking you why you have never married?

Ah, it is to be one of those evenings. I can feel it already. However, I do wish that man would stop taking photographs. It makes me feel very conscious of my drinking. But what the hell ...

A: Because I have never met anyone as delightful as you.

Flatter her with schmaltz to begin with. God, she's even blushing at that dire platitude. How avant-garde can you get?

Q: No, seriously—is it because you dislike the idea of marriage?

A: How can I answer that—I am not married. It is often too easy for the bachelor to criticize marriage because of what he sees around him. I have never understood and nobody has ever convincingly explained to me what the true purpose of marriage is. To an outsider, it strikes me as being rather anachronistic in this modern age, and slightly masochistic. Are you married?

Q: No.

A: Then *you* answer the question. It is more your domain. Especially in this country. To most women, especially the unambitious, the only life worth living is other people's. That's why they marry. To me, the only life worth living is my own. That's why I haven't.

Q: That sounds terribly selfish.

A: Do you expect me to be perfect?

Q: No, but surely there is more to marriage than that? Children for instance.

A: But I have two children.

Q: Oh.

That stopped her and allows me time to fill the glass. I am in a nonsense mood and in no mind to be rational. If she believes I am honest, then she is as much a fool as she makes out.

Q: Can we change the subject?

She is. She is. Ah well ...

Q: Have you ever seen a happy marriage?

A: I thought we were changing the subject?

Q: Well—

A: I don't know if I have seen a happy marriage. Husbands seem to delight in exhibiting the misery, and wives in exhibiting the pleasure. Both are biased. All I know is that I realized quite suddenly long ago that wives of my friends disliked me intensely. It was the beginning of my persecution complex which I enjoyed for a while, until I wasn't invited to dinner any more.

Q: I am sure there must be many wives who would be only too glad to invite you to dinner.

A: Ha! ha!

I wish the bitch would go.

Q: May I ask you your description of the perfect woman?

A: I have never met such a freak and never want to.

Q: Well then, how would you describe your ideal woman? Would she be beautiful?

If she expects me to talk about you, Antonella, rest assured I won't. Oh, why did I suddenly remind myself of your face? Perhaps it's the bourbon. Shall I have another?

A: Beautiful perhaps. No, beautiful of course. They unfortunately have the hardest time, and that is why I adore them even more. Women despise them, cowards are frightened of them, old men misunderstand them, queers adopt them, egotists exhibit them, the rich rape them, the poor ogle them, and the middle-class never marry them. They are denied a brain and if they haven't they are exploited, and then, at thirty, they are condemned. Beautiful women in my experience are the unhappiest of them all. I don't give a damn for the wailings of the plain girl. She will get her apron and kids before too long. The average man is pathetically insecure and so scurries to the altar with his mother's image nailed to the girl next door. I would rather know the man who has been married five times to the beautiful, than the pedant who is still married to the plain. I do not bring love into this. I talk of marriage. And marriage today has nothing whatsoever to do with God or society. If you think it has, then you are not only a hypocrite, you are also a bore.

Q: Do you really believe that? It sounds monstrous.

A: Don't forget it is you who labelled me an outsider and a non-conformist. If you call someone a dog, why should you be surprised if he barks?

Q: But not all beautiful women are sad victims as you say. I have met —

You cow. Just because you're fat and your room-mate has all the dates.

A: No, of course not. Most though. There are times however when they deserve what they get. I have seen hundreds of women who appear at parties or whatever and who exhibit only the physical side of themselves. They spend hours in the beauty parlour and under the drier. They scrape to buy the latest fashions. They pimp and preen their skin and their body in order to look as sexually attractive as possible. They offer nothing more than that, and yet when a man takes the very thing they exhibit, they complain he is only after their body. What fools! They have never even hinted they had anything else. Those women I never feel sorry for. I merely fuck them. Will you print that?

Q: I—don't—

A: Is your editor a man?

Q: No ...

A: You won't.

Another drink. The photographer I notice is actually composing the caption and shaping the gossip. 'Lecher and lush at the St Francis' I can see it now. Well, what has his petty life got above mine? Perhaps, though, he is contented. Oh, no—the room has just tilted. Not yet. Not yet ...

Q: You mentioned—are you all right?

A: I was just looking for the ashtray.

Q: Oh. You mentioned God just then. It is well known that you are an atheist and have even been quoted as saying that you believe God is a myth.

A: Have I? If you say so.

Q: But you don't believe in God.

A: No. At least not in your God.

Q: What is that?

A: The God of a denomination. The priests' God. That is not mine.

Q: You don't accept the Catholic Church?

A: If it is based on the infallibility of the Pope, then I don't. Anyway, the man splits his infinitives.

Q: I do think you ought to treat the subject seriously.

A: But it's only serious to you. How can it be serious to me?

Q: Do you accept there is a heaven and a hell?

A: Such questions. No. It is too cut and dried.

Q: But there is purgatory.

A: Ah yes. That shows more understanding of man. It is obvious that God created heaven in a state of optimism, and hell in a state of pessimism. But that was too fanciful, and so He created purgatory in a state of panic.

My, I am being facetious. Oh dear, the bottle is empty. I will have to stand up and cross the room to get another. I can see them watching me now, exchanging glances. I might not even make it. I wonder why I am being so concerned … ?

A: Can we get off religion? It's very late and—

Q: What are your views on sex?

A: I have none. Nor should you. Nor should the damned legislator.

Q: You think perversion then should be—

A: There is only one perversion. And that is celibacy. I have to get some sleep now, so—

Q: Can I ask you one more question?

The bloody photographer has just poured me a drink and set it before me. The nerve of the man. I will refuse to drink it till he has gone. The interviewer has a piece of cigarette paper stuck on her lower lip. Ha ha.

A: All right. What is it?

Q: Don't you think your way of life is very immature? To me, it shows an almost infantile preoccupation, totally lacking in responsibility to society.

Oh, oh. I knew it. The American woman rears her bourgeois head once more. The guillotine might be messy, but it's very perceptive. Give her another five minutes and she and her Yale boy-friend will be calling me a communist. I'll smile and be naive.

125

A: You're right. I am immature and utterly irresponsible. But you see I have not been blessed by an American upbringing, and also I have a nasty habit of caring more for the individual than for society. I realize it is a tragic fault in my character, but if you show me how to climb on to the pedestal you have erected for yourself in the clouds, I may even lick your hand.

Q: Who on earth do you think you are?

A: Ravel.

Q: Ravel?

A: Yes. The music he wrote was beautiful.

She is gone. I am left alone. The room is empty. I cling on to the toilet and regain my balance, spilling the drink. Outside it is dark and across the square the neoned lights advertise airlines, and on the newstrip I see the word KENNEDY. *I am alone and full of self-pity. I sit on the bed. It is empty. The irony of it is absurd. Here I am, the notorious lecher. The envy of a million dreamers and I have no woman near me. I cannot even solicit in the streets for fear of being laughed at. I ought to be much too sophisticated for that. The phone doesn't ring since no one knows I am here. And even if they did, would they? I think of phoning Harriette but it is too late for that. We have finished and my pride ... I stare at the ceiling. I even miss Catesby, and if he entered the room now I would offer him a drink and pat the cushions. He seems very close to me somehow. Right at this minute. I ought to go out.*

An hour later, the ceiling is around my ears. I have made a few phone calls hopefully, but wives have answered. Or husbands.

I decide to take a walk as the evening is reasonably fine and go down to the lobby. I notice a few hard stares and back-of-hand comments from the staid flock sitting in the centre of the foyer, but I ignore them and controlling my unbalance I push through the revolving door. For a brief instance I catch my reflection in the glass and look away startled. The eyes that look back at me cannot be my own. These eyes are lost, bewildered and pitiful. Lines are heavy around the mouth and the chin is unshaven. And the hair is as limp as the collar of the shirt. Perhaps, if I hurried, I could catch that photographer and burn his film.

Outside, I notice Benson the chauffeur, sitting in my car. I realize that I forgot to dismiss him, and walk towards him. Then suddenly I stop and wonder if *he* knows of some women. He might even pick one up for me. The thought staggers my ego and I brush it aside. And yet, I am sitting next to him in the front seat (much to his surprise) and offering him a cigarette.

'I'll leave the evening in your hands, Benson,' I say. 'Go wherever you like. I'll just ... tag along.'

He stares at me in surprise and I see he is embarrassed. For a moment he fumbles with the key.

'How—how do you mean, sir?' he asks painfully.

'Well, you know—I'm always dictating to you. I thought for once, that you could ... you know? I'll even drive if you like and you can sit in the back and wave out of the window.'

He knows I'm drunk. He can tell that. But that is not new to him. I see him sit confused, staring through the windscreen. For a moment, I believe he is dead. Then he turns back to me, helpless, and frowns like a baby.

'I ... I couldn't let you do that, sir. Drive I mean ... '

'Why not? I have a licence.'

'I know, sir ... but I'll go off on my own. I'd feel embarrassed sitting in the back ... '

'Don't be a fool, Benson.'

'No, sir ... '

He shakes his head painfully.

'All right. *You* drive then. I thought I was doing you a favour. Apparently not.'

I slam open the glove compartment and take out a flask. Benson has refilled it. He does it as often as he refills the car. Sometimes, more. I drink thirstily, aware of the confusion beside me. Benson is a Cockney, from West Ham, and like all Cockneys has a pathological fear of any class that is above him. Outside his own boundaries, he is totally lost and a little afraid. It is only the rebel who moves successfully out of the East End, though in the process he too acquires a class consciousness. But it is reversed and even worse. Benson is not a rebel. He is a servant and he always will be. That is his ambition and not even you can change it. The scar is too deep.

'Start the car then, Benson,' I shout with a hint of jollity. 'Let's get moving.'

'Yes, sir.'

The Rolls eases away from the palm-fronted entrance to the St Francis, and tours slowly round Union Square. After the third circuit, I ask with a sigh:

'Is this the best you can do, Benson?'

'I wondered where you wanted to go, sir.'

'Where *you* want to go, Benson. Where *you* ... It is your evening.'

He is now tongue-tied. Perhaps this is a bad idea after all. But no, I will stick it out. I am not often stubborn, but tonight ...

'Tell me, Benson, what do you usually do when you are on your own? For an evening?'

'Well ... I sometimes go to the pictures.'

'You go to the pictures. And?'

'Well, then again I may just take a look around the town, sir. See what's about.'

He's relaxing now. I try and remember his first name.

'Anything else?'

'Well ... I might just go and have a drink.'

'Just a drink?'

'Or two, sir.'

'Three even. Anything else?'

'Well ... not really.'

'What about women?'

'Oh, well ... ' He grins, embarrassed. I smile and humour him. Men-of-the-world act.

'Tell me, what kind of women do you like? Big ones with huge tits or do you go for the thin ones?'

'Well, sir. It depends. I mean, I'm not in your class, sir.'

'They're all the same underneath,' I joke and he laughs loudly.

'Timothy, isn't it?'

'Thomas, sir,' he replies. 'Thomas.'

'Well, Tom, what do you prefer? American girls?'

'Oh no, sir. Too bossy for me. I don't know why, though. Most of them are slags.'

'Are they now? Well, well, Tom, you *have* been around. I'm sure you could teach me a few tricks.'

The car is now on its fifth circuit. Union Square is beginning to seem almost like home. Benson is now very much at ease. I offer him the flask but he declines with a gesture to the car, and I nod.

'Do you fancy a woman tonight, Tom?'

'Well ... I'd never turn it down. Wouldn't kick it out of bed, as they say.'

'Do they now? Well, let's see if we can find one for you,' I lie to him. *He* may pull the creature, but it will be against my wall she will stand.

'Well, I ... '

'Don't be shy, Tom. I'm sure there are plenty of adorable girls in San Francisco who will want you. We could try Grant Avenue. Do you like Chinese?'

'Too small for me.'

'Yes, they usually are. Rather good in bed, though most of them snore.'

'Is that a fact, sir?'

'That's a fact. Look, just for fun, let's drive around and look at the clubs. Might find something there for you. I'd hate to think you were being deprived.'

Benson is unsure but I laugh once more and nudge his arm. The car stops circuiting, and the engine is switched off. I turn with a grin to him and reach for the door. But I am stopped by an indecision, almost a fear in his eyes. And then, inevitably, he looks away embarrassed.

'I ... I don't think I ought to go, sir,' he says finally. 'If you don't mind ... '

His voice is quiet, flat and pleading. For a moment, I feel like shouting at him, but I know I'm wrong. The man has a conscience and I am not yet, not quite yet, a devil. I nod sympathetically.

'Do you love your wife, Tom?' I ask, placing the cross on my own shoulder.

'Well ... I don't know about love, sir. But ... well ... she is my wife.'

I begin to loathe myself. I have made the man, and an honest man at that, feel ashamed. It's too easy. Much too easy. Father of two, husband of one.

'Well, I suppose it isn't such a good idea after all,' I say, 'and I ought to have an early night.'

Neither of us move or say a word for a full minute. We stare at a trolley that lurches past and then disappears over the rim of Powell Street. We are both paralysed.

'Good night, Tom,' I add, and open the door. He

doesn't look at me or even reply. In his wallet no doubt there lies a photo of his family taken in the back garden. They always are.

I cross the road back to the hotel and climb the steps. The commissionaire tips his hat to me and I smile. A girl walks by, utterly absorbed by her own entity, and he gives me a wink and a leer. I stare through him, hating the man, and hurry to my room. The bourbon still lingers in my head but I no longer crave a physical release. I am getting old. Thirty-seven only perhaps, but the age itself is immaterial. I am just getting old.

Without bothering to turn on the light, I stand at the window and gaze down at the Rolls still parked below. Benson hasn't moved. Tomorrow I will sit once more in the back of the car and he will speak not a word. I will conveniently forget his first name and I will complain if he goes too fast. He, in his turn, will avoid my eye and press his uniform. There will be few smiles. I turn away and remind myself to fire him by Friday. It is the only thing I can do.

As I begin to undress, the phone rings. A woman's voice, rather hesitant, quotes a friend of a friend who is utterly unknown to me. No matter. I tell her to come round immediately. She is there within the hour. She is middle-aged and hideously fat, and has brought her pet chihuahua. When we are all within the sheets, I jokingly suggest a little game. She will call me Pinocchio, and I on my part, just for the fun of it, will call her Antonella. The whore agrees with an apathetic shrug.

*   *   *

There are thousands of people around me. They fill the horizon and trample on me. I am in Elsinore under its green copper roof, and in the pits of destruction, grovelling in the mud. My face is stained with slime and I recognize the eyes and ears of creatures beneath me as they drown silently. A Negro child cleans my shoes with his mouth and I ask his name but he runs away. The room is as small as a box and a cockroach the size of a farmer's kitten snuggles up within my loins. Beside me, a child discovers the body of his mother in a meadow. I try to scream but the sound is dead, and when the bottles are all empty I lie quivering above the deserts until the eighth day. And it is now quiet. I walk in Central Park amid squirrels and the clean shun me.

In my room, I listen to Purcell and find I am quoting poetry I never remember reading. The alcohol gouges out my eyes. On the tenth day I realize at last that I am insane, and the banging on the shutters ceases. I become sober at last and I trim my hair and even eat some food. I must be in New York. Ah yes, I am. Never mind. It isn't so bad. Besides, it's my birthday. I am thirty-eight years old today. How come you never sent me a card?

*   *   *

I must confess it was quite a shock when I was told I was almost bankrupt. I had never realized I had spent so much, but I am assured I had. It is quite obvious I never had a head for figures, and what didn't go on tax, went on squalor. In those past nineteen years, I have toured the world twice (Bangkok is rather sweet. You ought to go there), and have lived in the very best of styles. I can't say I have ever been really happy, but the years went by without too much fuss, and though the details have long since gone, I do feel it wasn't all completely wasted. Sometimes I wish I had read a bit more, and perhaps learnt a language or two, but on the whole I am not regretful.

I'm glad I was thirty-eight in New York. Somehow I feel at home in the city. The people there are as narrow-minded as the rest of the country, but they tend to be much more tolerant of the eccentric. And I suppose, in my own small way, I *am* an eccentric. Of course, I can move my elbows in London, but it's not the same city now. It's much too self-conscious. I have never cared for the impolite sycophancy exhibited by waiters and hangers-on, and in London it is becoming embarrassing. They're even doing it to *tailors* now. Society there seems to be composed entirely of people who feed you, dress you, pose for you and entertain you. It's the rise of the servant class with a bitter vengeance. The masters, the professionals and the wits are now relegated to the wings, abandoned, shut out and supremely enviable. No, I'm relieved, I emerged from my week-long binge and found myself in New York.

When I realized I was thirty-eight as well, I decided I ought to celebrate the fact. I had been invited to innumerable parties, but I declined most of them. All the women there were mere children, and I would never find Antonella amongst that lot. Anyway, she must be easily thirty-four by now, and more likely to be found touring the museums or choosing gloves in Bonwit Teller. She wasn't, because I looked and bought an umbrella. Anyway, to return to the celebration. I figured an orgy was more in keeping with my character. They're usually very dull and painfully giggly, but with a little bit of luck I could instil a few outrageous fireworks into the proceedings.

And so, I planned the affair for the Wednesday. ORGY, I wrote on the invitation cards. DRESS OPTIONAL. And then I ordered fifty bottles of Moet Chandon '59 and a bag of olives and covered the floor of the suite with cushions. (I also hid my best towels.) It was to be my last extravagance (my money was now down to three figures in sterling) and so had to be lavish. I chose the music with care (Bartok to begin with, and a selection of popular favourites, followed by something on the sitar and then strings), and sprayed the room with perfume. Naturally, no one turned up. Who wants to go to an orgy on Wednesday—especially at the Plaza?

So I ended up with two young girls someone had recommended. They were twins, I understand, and very pretty. They had never heard of me but that didn't bother them. Usually, I don't have a penchant for two girls at once. Not because I am a prude, but simply because it is rather difficult to satisfy all at the same time, and there always seems to be one leg too many. Most double acts (or *Fleurs de Lys* as they are known in the trade) are usually performed by women who are either slightly lesbian or ridiculously narcissistic, so that they spend more time touching each others' bottoms than in entering into the true spirit of the thing. Unless you are a voyeur, it can be rather boring. But on that particular Wednesday, I didn't mind. It was frivolous and fun and a pretty escape, and afterwards one of them made coffee.

The next day, Harriette phoned when I was out. I didn't call back.

On the Friday, Catesby turned up, and on the Saturday I went to the zoo.

10

The last few pages are all lies. It is obvious that they are. I have never read such sentimental rubbish. I must have been drunk when I wrote it. I mean, some of it is so pathetic, I would expect it to be the ravings of a beggar like Catesby, and not someone like me. I ask you therefore to ignore all that self-pitying bilge you have just ploughed through, and allow me to remind you of my true character. I don't give a damn for sentiment, and nor should you, and each morning I tell myself how loathsome people are, especially women, and resolve to act accordingly. Yield to your fellow man and you are a fool. Catesby was that. He was a fool and a romantic madman.

I remember the last time I saw him, nineteen years ago. I was driving fast out of a small town in France (I forget the name), and I remember it was raining. About a mile from the town, there were the ruins of an old monastery on a hill. It was quite a landmark and I do believe it appears in the *Michelin Guide*. Well, I was just passing by the place, and I must have been doing about eighty miles an hour, when I could have sworn I saw him standing in the ruins. At first I couldn't believe it, of course. But then I stopped the car and crept out into the pouring rain to get a closer look. It was Catesby all right. And he was standing in his best suit singing—can you believe it? Singing!—while the rain soaked him to the skin. The song was one of those Music Hall numbers Dan Leno made famous. Naturally, I was stunned, but not really *very* surprised. After all, Catesby had been behaving peculiarly ever since Zordar and I could see that his insane pre-occupation with God and his own guilt-ridden soul was doing him no good. I tried to warn him many times, of course, being a man of the world. But he wouldn't listen. The pathetic bastard. He never did forgive me for sewing those drawing pins into his trousers. I wish I had sewn them into his lungs.

That, then, was the last time I saw him. I thought perhaps he had died. I even *hoped* he had. But that wasn't the case. Catesby was still alive, though at first I hardly recognized him.

It was on a Friday as I mentioned. I was sitting on the balcony of the suite, eating my breakfast. It was a warm day and it seemed rather pleasant. Moreover, it gives me a fine feeling of superiority as I stuff my stomach with muffins, and gaze down at all those grubs in Central Park who are feeding the ducks or sitting in the empty ice rink or other such wretched behaviour. I turn my thumb down at them, and now and again I flick an egg-soaked soldier of toast over the parapet and watch it drop on to the people below. And once, for a little quiet fun, I stripped a girl naked and left her out there on the balcony all day. I remember I went to see a film called *L'Avventura* and fell asleep, and when I woke up and left the cinema, I noticed that it had been raining. This amused me since the girl would at least have had a wash. She was, quite rightly, blue with cold, but strangely very seductive, since her skin was smeared with grime and her hair stuck to her head. I made love to her on the spot, then gave her a cup of cocoa and an orange. Her name, by the way, is Emily and she has an aunt in Wyoming who ought to be more careful.

On this particular Friday, however, there was no Naughty Nellie sharing my breakfast. Instead, I had chosen to eat alone, and was idly perusing the gossip columns in the *New York Post*. I had been to a dreary Show Business party the night before, and a bore from the coast had decided to put his hand up my partner's skirt and grope her knickers. He was married, of course, and drunk. The incident had got into Earl Wilson's column (together with a rather constipated photo of the girl) and was occupying me during the orange juice. It was then that I heard the sounds of bands and of people singing.

'What's that noise?' I remarked to the waiter as he poured out the coffee.

'A parade, sir.'

'A parade?'

'Yes, sir. On Fifth Avenue. Polacks.'

Ah, a Polish parade. Extraordinary—how New Yorkers adore parades. I had never actually seen one since I have a dislike for crowds, but on this day I felt rather in the mood. It would take my mind off my financial problems, which had begun to pester me. For the past week, the phone had been plagued with the whining voices of debtor and accountant, until I ordered the hotel switchboard to leave me alone. Take the damn thing away.

'How long does it last?'

'About four hours, sir. Maybe five. There's an awful lot of Polacks in this town.'

I was dressed and in the street in no time. It was packed with people and already I could see the heads of trumpeters and hear the distant rumblings of bass-drums. Police barriers had been set up along the kerb edges, so that the crowds were pressed together and walking was difficult. In no time it was impossible. I don't know from where I inherited my claustrophobia, but often it proved a damnable irritation. My father never suffered from it, I am sure, for he spent most of his life shut up in darkened rooms making love to rejects and cripples. Apparently, I have two or three half-brothers somewhere, but I don't want to meet them, and if they dare to come near me, I'll cut them dead. That's a promise.

Before long, what with the noise and the crowds pushing and elbowing, I began to feel a slight panic rising within me. I tried to run but I was hemmed in by grinning faces, and small children seemed to be clinging to my shoes. The noise grew louder and I began to feel wave upon wave of crushing music which seemed to reach a pitch of nausea. I wanted to hurry on to the road itself, but I was blocked by the barriers, and the people were now becoming aware of my anxiety and were staring and whispering remarks. I could hear them. Whispering remarks and poking fingers into my eyes. I turned, I turned and thrust myself against the wall of the shops, against the surface of the rock, and I could hear the buzz threading through my brain. The drums and the legs of majorettes and visions of nuns on the high balconies above me. I had to get away. I threw myself into darkness, and found myself alone and bathed in an immediate blissful peace.

I wasn't sure where I was at first, but it was dark and very quiet and the sounds of the parade were muffled and far away. Slowly, my eyes grew accustomed to the gloom, and I realized I was in a church. St Patrick's no doubt. I was in a church and despite my hatred of God I was thankful for the first time for its sanctuary. It was a strange sensation, alien to me, and yet not unfamiliar. It seemed to stir out of my childhood. I remember I stood in the aisle of the church for a long time, till the shivering in my body had stopped and I was breathing more easily. Often people passed by, but only a few and they didn't jostle me or peer into my eyes, or pull at my tie. Finally, I turned to go, my confidence regained. It was then that I saw him. He was sitting in one of the pews, staring at me. It wasn't an impolite stare that one would give to a freak or a celebrity, but rather an observance. I know the word is odd, but it is the best I can do. He was merely observing me, quite calmly and without any ulterior motives. I didn't recognize him at once, because he'd changed a lot. Oh, I admit that shocked me — the change. His hair was almost gone and he'd put on a great deal of weight. Even from this distance and in this light I could make out heavy lines under the eyes and deep creases around the neck. I assumed he was almost fifty but he looked much older. I can't say what exactly betrayed his identity. Perhaps it was the mouth (that unique lazy M of the upper lip), or maybe it was just the expression, or the angle of the body. Perhaps in fact it was none of these. How rarely can one remember visually the facial details of even one's closest friends. If one has any. But it was Catesby all right. C-for-Charlie Catesby. A sad wreck of what I remember, but, yes, it was Catesby.

I looked away immediately, hoping he hadn't recognized me, and when I looked back, he was gone. I peered around the church, but he was nowhere to be seen. I shrugged it off and left the church. The parade was still there but my mind was no longer on it. All I wanted was a large bourbon and I was going to get it in the first bar I reached. It wasn't far.

When I emerged, two hours later, only the garbage remained in the streets. It was still light and I would have stayed in the place longer but I was forced out by a bore. The man cornered me in the bar and regaled me with endless anecdotes of his callousness towards women. This annoyed me, not because of his impertinence or the philosophy he was propounding, but because he thought I would be interested. And so when I eventually reached the street, I felt decidedly better and in quite a good mood, and even eager to stroll back to the hotel. Then I saw him again. He was sitting in the back of a Chequered Cab and he was watching me. I only caught glimpses of him as the car sped by, but he was definitely watching me. He must know who I am. Even if he didn't read the papers he would have recognized my face. I'm not *so* different. I dismissed him with a loud expletive that startled a passer-by, and hurried down Fifth Avenue, abandoning any idea of a simple promenade. I was annoyed that such a creature could spoil my temper, and even more annoyed that I should be so concerned. Why didn't he speak, or even wave? I am not an ogre. A monster.

At the hotel, I went straight to my room and ordered a bottle of Old Grandad, some ginger and another bucket of ice. One glass. When it arrived, I was presented with a polite concentration of thought by the bell-boy. I figured that like all healthy boys of his age, he was simply stoned out of his mind, but this in fact was not the case. The switchboard operator had told the cashier who had told the desk clerk, who had passed it on to the bell-captain who had distributed it among his catamites that my finances were in a shaky state. Somebody had been eavesdropping, and this particular bell-boy (I do wish they wouldn't give me *green* jiggers) had realized that his tip at the end of my stay might well be non-existent. I outstared him and gave him nothing whatsoever, and even complained about the ice.

When he had gone, I sat in silence and stared at the wall. There were bills in the waste-paper basket and it looked as if my financial state was becoming serious. I had never really worried about money before. It had always been there (my father had left me a sizable amount when he died), and there seemed no end to it. Apparently there *was* an end and it was in sight. I refused to find out how much because that would really depress me, but I will say again, the matter was serious. I know you don't give a damn anyway, and I'm sure I won't be seeing your simpering face mouthing Hello to me across Orsini's now that I'm on the way to the dogs. Who needs you? I'm quite happy to drink alone. Cheers.

*   *   *

The manager is becoming difficult. Apparently my last cheque bounced. I told him it was an oversight on my part, and that I had forgotten I had transferred my account from the First National to the Chemical Bank because I preferred the name. I think he believed me. After all, my reputation as a man of wealth is still intact. So is my other reputation, I am very relieved to say. The avant-garde interview came out last week, and I think I emerged from it rather well. The photograph of course was abysmal. I looked at least ten years older and slightly gay of all things. On top of that, I am described by the writer as being *hypergenitally-minded*. Hypergenitally-minded? What the hell is that? It's an odd phrase to say the least. I had to look it up. Apparently *hypergenitalism* is a state characterized by excessive development of the sex organs. She is in fact telling her readers that I am slightly over-sexed. Well, perhaps I am, but there's no need for *her* to be shy about it.

But all in all, the article was not so bad, and since it was known that I was in New York, the women soon came round after reading it. The procedure is the same all over the world — except of course in France or Italy where they know nothing whatsoever about sex, and even less about women. Anyway, to come back to the women visitors and their techniques. Almost all of them were housewives, who invented ridiculous lies in order to get into my suite. I never knew I had so many sisters and cousins, and one bitch even called herself my daughter. No one believed them of course, least of all me, and after the initial reluctance (fifty-five seconds on the outside) they were in the bed and releasing what seemed to be their first orgasm in years. They invariably told me afterwards of their husbands, who were called John or Bill (and, surprisingly, Alan is very common), and most show me a photo of their son. They are all shy of their nakedness, mainly because they are ashamed of their figures and anxiously cover paunches, pitted thighs and veined breasts with anything that comes to hand. Their visits were always during the day (three till four was popular), and before leaving they all insisted on tidying up the room and washing the dishes. My name was never uttered by them, nor was any interest shown in me whatsoever, other than as a lover. And when they had gone and I was left alone, I was sure to find their Christian name (surname in brackets) and their number underneath, followed by the safe times to call, underneath the butter dish.

I collected seventeen of these in the past fortnight, plus a Sue and a Jill and a Celia and a Lynn, who were all nineteen years old, and like all pretty girls of nineteen incredibly bad in bed. I should have realized it when they arrived. Two called themselves actresses (whatever *they* are), one was a model, and the other was an American debutante. Now, I have long discovered that the last creature I want in my bed is a model. Her impersonation of rigor mortis during the act of sex no longer amuses me. The actress and that freak, the deb, are little better, though the latter seems to insist on shouting out 'God!

God! God!' during the performance which annoys me intensely, since that is not my name. Yet.

But they are all gone now. I am growing tired of them all. I have found myself studying my face in the mirror with much more frequency than is usual. I am not pleased with what I see. The signs are there, and recently I have been aware of my failing energy and demands for sleep. Coupled with poverty and the sight of Catesby, it has not been a very good month. I am becoming more and more depressed, and can only think of one thing that would lift me out of this swamp.

*   *   *

ANTONELLA — need you desperately. Remember our Verona — C. Write Box M38.

*   *   *

But there were no replies. I didn't really expect them, but it was a hope. Perhaps I'll place the same ad in the London *Times* and *France-Soir*. One never can tell. I found a photograph of her hidden in the pages of an old book. I thought I had lost it for ever. It was taken when we visited Rimini. She is standing in an orchard and is just staring into the camera. It is very simple and very sweet. I remember it amused us both a great deal, because by an odd combination of the light and her pose the dress she is wearing seems to hang very strangely. It makes her look as if she is pregnant, which of course is ridiculous.

Anyway, I'm glad I found it, and will keep it in a safe place. I also discovered an old address book, which kept me fascinated for hours. It must be at least fifteen years old, and most of the names are either English or French. Ah, this one is interesting. Fiona. I still remember her, surprisingly. I see I only gave her one star. And Janine. And one girl called Felicity who was given four stars, then demoted to three. I wonder what she did right? Extraordinary how faces come back to one. Most of them, naturally, I have forgotten, but some still linger. Jane. I remember her. She never went to bed without the trace of a tear on her cheek. That was the way she was. Without that, she could never sleep a wink. I recall she had a sister called Marian who had got so used to being on the shelf she refused to come down. 'I'm going to paint it maroon,' she would cry with smothered glee. 'That's what I'm going to do.'

I spent a good hour reading the book. And then I looked at Antonella's photograph. My mind in fact became so incensed with visions of her that I went out and bought a canvas and some paints and actually painted a picture of her. Would you believe it? It was something I hadn't done since I was a boy. But then I suddenly had this urge to paint her. It was a nude study in the Impressionist manner. She is lying on her stomach (it was originally her back, but breasts are terribly hard to draw from memory. The nipples always seem to be in the wrong place), and is on a rock. Her face is almost obscured by her hair, which is blonde and reaches almost halfway down her back. I have put little realistic touches in, like the un-tanned strip across her back and the triangle over her bottom where her bathing costume would be. I think the picture is rather good and I might even frame it. I haven't yet settled on the title, but am toying with 'Nude on a Rock' or 'Composition in Beige and Grey', or whatever. I'll think of something.

*   *   *

I woke up this morning in a cold sweat. I had forgotten her name. I had forgotten it. Her name.

11

The magazine is in my briefcase. Every now and then I peek inside and make sure it is still there, and once or twice I even take it out altogether and lay it on my lap. I am sure the passenger on my right thinks I'm insane, but I don't care. It's only a small photograph, four by three at the most, and I wouldn't have noticed it at all if I hadn't needed a haircut. It was the only magazine in the place, you see, and normally I don't read news magazines because they are always so dull. But since I was bored, and the barber had almost nothing intelligent to say, I picked it up and idly glanced through it. On page 41 I stopped, and almost lost part of my ear. On the bottom left-hand corner, smuggled into a feature entitled MODERN LIVING, was a rather smug photograph of a man and a woman at a fashion show. They were just sitting watching this fashion show. He was English and rather distinguished, I suppose, and I would think he was about forty years old. Thirty-nine to forty. Next to him was a very attractive woman in her early thirties, who, it appeared, was his wife. She was looking straight into the camera, her chin tilted slightly, her eyes half-closed, and had the features and poise of a sensual aristocrat. I have met her equivalent only a dozen times in my life, and each time I have been enchanted. One remembers her in the fireglow of her child's bedroom, as she sits in her satin ball gown, reading *Winnie the Pooh* to a sleepy youngster, while a band plays an early waltz in the hall below and guests gossip on the stairs. She is the woman who occupies the suite above you in that hotel in

Cap Ferrat, and who, arms folded, head at an angle, tours the Turner collection in the Tate Gallery every other Wednesday. She is usually married to an industrialist, and lives either in an English country house surrounded by dogs and Chippendale, or in its counterpart in Austria or Sweden.

This woman in the photograph was like that. I could tell, and I must confess I was not surprised. The caption underneath described them as Mr and Mrs Meredew, but that was only a formality. The husband I recognized immediately. I'd met him two or three times in London, at Crockford's, and once he gave me a lift to Henley. I knew little about the man except that there was something rather false about him, and that his name was Peter or Edward. I knew he was married but had never met his wife. He had talked about her but had failed to mention her name. I could supply it now. I could supply it now to the bastard. This pathetic, chinless, throw-up of English phlegm has gone off and married my Antonella. He has gone out into the night and stolen my own sweet Antonella. I'm going to pay them both a visit. I'm going to surprise them. Oh, God, why are my legs trembling like this? Can't you keep them still?

It's rather a fine aeroplane, though I do think the journey is very dull. Naturally I cannot sleep or read, and my yearning to see A. again, coupled with my fear of flying, is hardly doing my composure justice. The hostess has been very kind and has supplied me with endless champagne. I tried to tell her about A. but she didn't understand, poor thing.

'I'm going to collect her in London,' I told her, 'then we're flying off to the Mediterranean. Just the two of us.'

'What part of the Mediterranean is that, sir?'

147

'It'll be a reunion, you see. We haven't seen each other for nineteen years. *Nineteen* years.'

'I always feel Italy is very romantic. Have you been there, sir? All those mandolins.'

'She hasn't changed. She's still as beautiful as ever. Of course she would be.'

'Just press the button above your head if you need anything, sir.'

'It was worth the waiting. I must have looked in a million cities for her, and there she was. In the magazine. This one. *Time*. Here. There she was. I was sitting in the barber's chair and I couldn't believe it. First plane out. Oh, yes. I'm a man of impulse. I took the first plane ... out. I'm going to surprise them. They don't know I'm coming. I'm going to arrive unexpectedly for tea. She'll be out in the garden collecting a forgotten book, and I'll ... appear. From nowhere. I will. After all those years—'

'Yes, sir?'

'Who are you?'

'Miss Taylor. I'm the hostess, sir. You rang the bell. Is there anything you require?'

'Yes—why are all those people staring at me?'

*   *   *

I drove down. I hired a car in London from Avis and drove down to the house. It was in Oxfordshire, in a small village and only just on the map. It was a fine day, sunny and warm, and so I hired a sports car, a Triumph, because it had only two seats. One for her and one for me.

English countryside is breathtaking. I realize I have English blood in my veins, but that doesn't bias me. There is nothing finer in the world than the quiet beauty of England. It doesn't arrogantly attack you with its splendour like the Grand Canyon or the columns of Italy, nor does it smugly sneer at you like the landscape of France. It just waits for you to gaze at it, and to dream. I never tire of driving along those lanes, miles from anywhere, stopping only for a beer at a good-natured pub, or to watch a pony being exercised by a young girl. It was these distractions alone that kept my stomach in one piece, though I must admit I was grateful for the English drinking laws or I would have been upside down and in a ditch if I hadn't been stopped.

When I arrived at Meredew's house, it was about five in the afternoon. The building was just off the road and seemed rather austere. As I drove slowly up the drive to its door, I noticed a swimming pool at the back of the house, and a swing tied to an oak tree. Perhaps she has children? No, that couldn't be possible. That toy train lying on the lawn must belong to a neighbour. I parked the car on the gravel and got out. It was very still and there seemed to be no one around. Slowly, I walked to the side door (one always enters English country houses by the side door. That's why they are always open) and went inside.

I was in a large hall, dominated by a giant stone fireplace, in which shields were carved and animals from myths. On the stone floor before the fire were walnut shells and a slightly burnt cigarette packet. Somebody was obviously here. I called out a tentative Hello, but there was no reply.

Curious, I studied the hallway, then opened a door on my right. It was just a small cupboard. The next door however revealed a dining-room, reserved, it appeared, only for special occasions. A long table, eight high-backed chairs and a candelabra. A painting by Stubbs on a wall. Good taste. I like the tapestry and someone has chosen just the right curtains. I called out again. Nothing.

Soon, I was walking boldly through the house, opening doors without apprehension, and even whistling. The ground floor consisted of the dining-room, a rather grand sitting-room and two smaller rooms besides kitchen and hall. In each one, the decor was superb, though you must realize that it wasn't the decor I sought. I found one photo of her on a desk in the study, and it reconfirmed my anxiety. She had indeed become a beautiful woman, though her eyes don't seem as clear as I remember. By the letters in the drawer (I spent a heart-stopping fifteen minutes glancing through them), it was obvious her husband didn't deserve her. He never mentioned her name once.

I then walked upstairs, towards the bedrooms. The whole business was very strange, though I enjoyed the intrigue of it all. Here I am, in another man's house, sneaking into his private papers like a spy, preparing to poach his wife, and there is no one to stop me. There is no one even to wave me on. Where *are* they all? The master bedroom is there. I enter the room cautiously, and look at the bed and the dressing-table and the bed and shoes under the chair and the bed. No one is here. The over-all colour is green, which is restful I suppose, but hardly what I would want if I was in bed with Antonella. I wonder which side she lies on. This side? Would *she* be reading *Jane's Fighting Ships*? I lie down on the bed, where I believe she lies, and close my eyes, then open them again so that I can see the day as she sees it each morning for the first time. The window is seen first, then the flowers on the dressing-table. Her eyes perhaps flick to the ceiling now that she has established the mood, and she stares at that white plaster-moulded ceiling till her thoughts collect. Is her husband still in bed or has he gone to the office? Let us say he has gone. She gets up at last, and walks slowly towards the daylight. She is wearing a nightdress, no doubt. Only mistresses sleep naked in England. Her hand takes some clean underwear from this drawer (all white, I see. She can do no wrong), and wrapping this housecoat around her she walks to the bathroom which must be ... there. Yes. She showers. This nozzle and this tap have seen her naked, and so has this plastic duck, if that grin is anything to go by. It cannot be *her* plastic duck. And what about this third toothbrush by the basin? She must have a child. *A child!* Could it be? I hurry out of the bathroom and into the next room. It is a nursery and the toys are unbroken. A boy, of course, and at a guess he is six or seven. She has been married that long. I wonder how many affairs she has had. Seeking me, no doubt.

I pick up a plastic gun and walk to the window of the playroom. Below me, I can see the swimming pool and the rhododendrons and the lawn spreading away towards the woods. Beyond that, there is a row of hills and then blue sky. It is a warm day, reminiscent of the time when Antonella and I first met. I am beginning to grow excited, though slightly concerned at the absence of everybody, and turn to seek out the husband's wine cellar. As I do, I notice him. He is standing by the pool and seems to be intent on fixing a canopy over a seat. Obviously, my car hasn't been noticed, and so I duck away from the window before I am seen and hurry down to the hall again. There is only one thing for me to do, and that is to approach him directly. I cannot avoid it any longer. I therefore walk straight out into the garden and saunter casually towards him. Halfway there, he notices me and peers at me curiously. Obviously I am not yet recognized, and he is slightly puzzled. I try to be more casual by putting my hands in my pockets, and discover I still have the plastic gun. It falls behind the lupins.

His face registers a scorefold of polite concern as I smile and assist him with the canopy.

'Nice day,' I remark, realizing I am in England.

He nods and looks at me out of the corner of his eye, then seems to find something hypnotic in the pool.

'I was just in the area, so I thought I'd drop by. See how you are.'

'Oh ... well, it's good to see you.'

He hasn't the faintest idea who I am, but he's so damned polite. I tease him.

'Fine house you have. Walter told me it was sixteenth century.'

'Walter?' he asks, frowning.

'Yes. Walter.' I know no one called Walter and nor does he. 'His wife left him. Of course it was inevitable. The bee-keeping, you know.'

'The ... bee-keeping?'

'Yes. Did you ever meet his wife, Meredew?'

He looks at me, startled, across the seat. I am now one up, for I have remembered his name. This naturally has embarrassed him. He coughs.

'Well ... no ... actually — Look, didn't we meet at ... ?'

I complete the clue:

'Crockford's.'

'Ah, yes.'

My eyes anxiously dart around the grounds and towards the windows of the house. Where is she? Where is my Antonella? I hold out my hand at last and I tell him my name. His gratitude is bound to promote an invitation to supper.

'How do you do?' I add.

He smiles and remembers me, and then, as if to cement the intimacy, points to a statue in the garden.

'Hermes.'

'Oh really?' I say, and we both stare at it in silence. It doesn't move.

'Brought it all the way from Kent.'

We walk round Hermes. He is completely naked, and well preserved for his age, though he appears to have been rather drastically circumcised by some butcher or other. Fig-leaves may be démodé, but they do protect one from unfortunate accidents in transit.

Perhaps Antonella has gone away. Oh no, she can't have.

'Isn't it rather a large house for just you to live in?' I ask casually, through the legs of the statue.

'Well, it's not *just* me. I mean, there's Ann. And William is here during the holidays.'

'Ann is your wife?'

'Yes. Haven't you met her? Oh. I thought you had. That's our duck pond over there. No ducks. Just geese.'

Ann. Ann. Ann-tonella. Why is he being so damned boorish and shortening her name? Ann. How awful.

'No, I never did. Is she—is she here?'

My heart races and I find the rockery diverting.

'No. She's out. You know what women are. Always—'

'Out?' I spin round, unable to control my horror. 'Out where?'

For a moment he looks at me, then I smile self-consciously and look away. He has noticed nothing. The English husband rarely does. One has to make love to his wife on his morning porridge before he even suspects something might be wrong. Foreigners therefore shrug and say that the Englishman ignores his wife's adultery because he is blind to it. Not at all. He ignores it because he is guilty. But he is guilty not of his own affairs (though he may have had one or two), but of his wife's. The Italians don't understand that. Nor do the French. But then, in Italy, the men marry their mothers, and in France they marry their mirrors. In England, however, the men (except for the middle-class android) usually marry their lovers.

'You mean—she's not here?' I ask as casually as is bearable.

Meredew strolls slowly towards the house.

'No. She left this morning to collect William from school. I think it's half-term or something. It always seems to be half-term. They should be back in an hour at the latest.'

An hour. Sixty minutes. She's on her way back here this minute. An hour. At the latest. One hour. By seven o'clock she'll be here. At the latest. Antonella—oh. I smile and compliment her husband ecstatically on the house. He is enormously flattered. I heap on more praise. I compliment everything. Everything I see. I even put in a good word for the dog.

'Good shooting country, this,' I say with absolutely no authority.

'Oh, very. Very. Damn good. Do *you* shoot at all?'

'No, I find poison more reliable.'

It's a terrible joke but he laughs. Why hasn't he asked me to supper?

We enter the house.

'I say—would you like to stay for supper? I'm not sure what Annie's got to eat, but I'm sure we can rustle up something. Do stay. She'd love to meet you.'

I do wish the man wasn't so nice. Perhaps I could push him in the duck pond.

'Well … I really ought to … ' I begin.

'Oh, please stay. We don't get many visitors dropping by. It would be nice to talk to somebody different besides each other.'

I hesitate suitably, then nod.

'All right. If you insist. But you're much too kind.'

'Think no more of it. Shall we have a drink? I have rather a nice whisky I've been waiting to open for months.'

I agree and follow him into the hall. As we are passing the fireplace, he stops to pat a spaniel that is asleep in the hearth.

'By the way, I hope you don't think I'm impertinent. But aren't you in electronics?'

'No,' I say.

'Oh, of course not. I must be mixing you up with someone else. I thought ... No, silly of me.'

A pause. And then the inevitable:

'What *do* you do?'

'I'm a lecher,' I reply sweetly. 'I steal other men's wives.'

There is a moment's intake of breath, then Meredew laughs loudly, until my name rings an even bigger bell and his face freezes sickeningly. I smile and pass it off as a joke and he relaxes slightly. Then with a grin he opens the door to the sitting-room. As I enter, I hear a car outside, approaching the house.

*   *   *

'Of course, we don't go to the theatre *that* much,' he is saying. 'Hardly at all really. What was the last thing we saw, darling? It was ages ago, wasn't it? It seems like ages ago.'

'*Henry the Fifth*. In Oxford.'

'Was it? I don't remember seeing it. Did *I* see it? *Henry the Fifth*? Must have been ages ago.'

'You didn't like it. You thought it was very noisy.'

We are on the brandy. A. is opposite me. Meredew is

on my right. The meal was delicious. I didn't touch a
scrap. I couldn't eat. We are in the special room. The light
is out. The candles are lit. She is exactly like the photographs. I am drunk. I don't listen. I just gaze, transfixed.
I yearn to be inside her mouth. I envy the tip of her
cigarette.

'Did I, Ann? Isn't that the one Robert was in? I'm sure
it was.'

'No, that was *Blithe Spirit*. Noël Coward. You never
saw it.'

'Oh. But I do think *Henry the Fifth* is awfully noisy.
I suppose Shakespeare wrote it as a plea for patriotism.
What do you think? Mmmm?'

I am suddenly aware that this grub on my right is
talking to me.

'I beg your pardon?'

'*Henry the Fifth*. Why do *you* think Shakespeare wrote
it?'

'Probably because the wardrobe at the Globe had
half a dozen tin swords and a cardboard crown left over
from *Henry the Fourth*,' I reply, my eyes fixed on hers.

She smiles. Perhaps I could set light to Meredew's tie.

'That's a very beautiful dress,' I say to her.

'Thank you,' she replies. 'It's the first time I've worn it.'

'You remind me of somebody I once knew long ago.'

'Does anyone want more brandy? Ann, darling, more
brandy?'

'No, thank you, Peter.'

'More brandy?'

I ignore him and carry on.

'I met her when I was eighteen.'

'First love?' she asks with a smile. She understands.

'Yes. It was in Yugoslavia. Have you been there?'

'Never. Is it nice?'

'Very. I'm thinking of going there tomorrow.'

'You must. If it means so much to you.'

We both drink. Meredew pushes his chair back loudly and stands up.

'Do you play snooker at all?'

'No,' I reply.

'No?'

'No. Nor billiards either.'

'What about chess? Do you have a penchant for chess by any chance?'

We both ignore him. He walks up and down ostentatiously, slapping one hand against his thigh. My eyes soothe the crease of his wife's breasts as it divides the triangle of her neckline. I notice her breathing.

'Stubbs. That's a Stubbs,' Meredew shouts. 'Did you see that? It's a ... '

His voice trails away, and he stares drunkenly into the air.

'What was her name?' she asks me. Her voice is soft.

'Antonella.'

'That's a beautiful name. I wish it were mine.'

'So do I,' I say. 'So do I.'

She looks away. There is a long silence. I refill the brandy glass and the noise is loud. After New York, the silence of the countryside deafens me.

'You live in Albany, don't you?' I am asked by her husband.

'No.'

'Yes you do. You live in Albany. I was positive you did.'

'No, I don't. The place reminds me of a baroque greenhouse filled with prized and rather precious blooms. It is ugly, tasteless and ignorant.'

'Oh. Well, I didn't mean it as an insult, old chap.'

His wife places her napkin on the table and gets up.

She is tall and fair and with a fine figure. It is *her* hand that has decorated the house. There is no doubt about that.

'Shall we go into the sitting-room, Peter? It's warmer there.'

'It's not cold,' he replies. 'Don't say you're cold. It's boiling.'

She leaves us alone. I stand up and pretend to admire the painting as I wait for him to speak. He grunts a few times nervously, then I hear his glass being refilled once more.

'I … suppose this must be a bit quiet for you. This place … '

'Not at all,' I say. 'Why should it be?'

'Well, you know. You and your playboy life. Ha ha! The stories I've heard about you. Tell me, what is—'

'May I have some more brandy?'

'Of course. Of course. Help yourself. Yes … I envy you. You and your freedom. No ties … '

I say nothing.

'Some of the women you've been out with … Well … I wouldn't mind being in your shoes just for a day. Know what I mean? And those comments in the papers. "Just good friends." Well, we all know what *that* means, don't we? Mmmm? Yes … Well, it's a bit more difficult for me, being married. But I don't say I don't have a little dabble. Keep this to yourself, but if my wife should see my secretary some day—well … Passes the lunch hour, don't you think? Ha ha! Better than food. Ha ha … '

I look at him with loathing and turn my back.

'That's what women are for, isn't it? You're a man of the world. *You* know that. Help yourself to some more brandy. Of course, Ann doesn't understand. Wives never do, do they? Tell me, have you ever had a nigger woman?'

158

Ah, how can the woman have married such a miserable wretch? So naive, so tragically naive.

'Of course, Ann's not *so* bad really. Could be worse. Could be a lot worse.'

Why are husbands always too embarrassed to praise their wives? That I can never understand.

'She's a beautiful woman,' I tell him. 'You're very lucky. I hope you realize it.'

He blushes slightly and gives a nervous laugh.

'Well, how come *you* have never married? Don't tell me you're still looking for your dream-girl?'

'Yes,' I reply, 'as a matter of fact, I am.'

A silence again, and then I walk out of the room. She is standing by the fireplace, lighting a cigarette.

'You have a fine son,' I tell her, staring into the fire.

'Yes. *I* think so.'

And then:

'Peter's never mentioned you before. I didn't realize he knew you.'

'We've only met once or twice. I was in the area, so I thought I'd just intrude on you.'

'But we're miles from anywhere.'

'So I discovered.'

I smile and take her hand.

'Well, it was nice meeting you. I ought to go.'

I can see a flicker of regret in her eyes, which holds me for a moment, but I cannot stay. The journey was a mistake. This isn't Antonella. She doesn't look a bit like her now, though she is very desirable and very lonely.

'We will see you again, won't we?' she asks quietly.

'I don't think so. By morning, I will be halfway to the Adriatic.'

I turn quickly and walk away. As I pass the dining-room, Meredew appears and calls out to me, but I just nod and leave without looking back. I have no excuse to make and I have no energy for lies.

His wife doesn't move from where she stands, until she hears the sound of the car start up and then roar away, and then silence. Her cigarette is thrown into the fire, as her husband approaches, staggering slightly, clutching a glass in his hand.

'Anything on telly tonight, then?'

She doesn't answer. She is wearing a new dress but he hasn't noticed. She too reaches for a drink.

'Darling?'

'Yes ... ?' she says quietly, not turning round. He is kneeling on the floor playing boisterously with the pet dog.

'See old Kaiser here. I swear his hair is getting more gingery. What do you think, darling? He's much more gingery than he was last week.'

He looks up, but she has taken a book and she has gone to bed.

*   *   *

The magazine is torn up and thrown out of the car. I must be blind. The photograph doesn't look a bit like Antonella. Whatever made me think it did? Besides, she wouldn't go and marry anyone. Of course she wouldn't. Not *my* Antonella. Not my A. Not her.

12

The events I am about to tell you are very close to me, as I lie here in my casket. I lie utterly alone here, my mind filled with thoughts. I wonder many times why I began this cautionary tale. It hardly comforts me, as I fade in darkness, and yet it is there. That woman's face, for example. Meredew's wife. It was only nine months ago when I sat opposite her at table and drank her husband's brandy. Nine months. And now I am in my coffin and I will never see anyone's face again, and soon, when the worms have finished, no one will ever see mine. That might sound morbid, but after death, it is not the body one cares about. It is the soul. Unfortunately, mine is still unclaimed. Yesterday, I heard a thump over me as the headstone was presumably placed in position. It didn't seem a very big one, though I am prepared to tolerate that, except for the fact that they've placed it over my feet.

I was saying that my life is now coming to a close. Remember, at the point we have just reached, I am thirty-eight years old, and rather a sad creature. No money, no friends, fading looks and little hope. I debated whether I ought to leave it at that, and ask you to close the book now, mainly to save me from my own terror. But after much deliberation, I realize I owe it to you to tell the macabre finale of this story, though I warn you, it is not pretty. But, as a small comfort, I will say that I come out of it worst of all, and I suppose, in a way, it was inevitable.

*   *   *

I think we'll skip the Yugoslavia trip. I've described it all before. Let me just say that I went there the next morning, went to the island and looked around. She wasn't there. It was raining. So I left and took a boat back to the mainland. Utter waste of time. I also caught a cold.

When I arrived back at Zordar, the rain had eased slightly, which was a blessing. A mist lay along the shore and in parts only the beach itself was visible. I could see the hotel where my father had died, and it hadn't changed. Someone had slapped a coat of blue over it, but it hadn't changed. I moored the boat by the jetty and began to walk along the beach towards the road. Soon, however, the journey became difficult as the mist settled close around me, and in no time I could barely see more than a few feet in front of me. I decided the best thing to do was to stop and work out my position. I listened, standing quite still on the sand, and I could hear the sea and the deep creaking of a boat. There was no other sound, not even of a car, which could guide my way to the road. I was lost. In this mist I could walk in circles for ever, so I decided the best thing to do was to wait till the air cleared, though I realized that might be hours.

Suddenly, a man appeared out of the gloom and approached me.

'Follow me,' he said, 'the road's just up there.'

'Thank you,' I replied. 'I was afraid I might be stuck here for hours.'

'Oh no. It's just up here.'

And so I followed him, and sure enough we were on the road within five minutes. Catesby must have eyes like a cat.

'Fancy meeting you here,' I said to him, as we sat in the bar of the hotel.

'Yes, it is rather a coincidence. I was visiting someone here, a sentimental journey, and I heard you had arrived and had gone out to the islands.'

'Yes. It was a sentimental journey for me too.'

'Oh really? Of course, this is where we first met,' Catesby said with a smile. He really did look old and very ill.

'Yes. Wasn't it?' I replied.

There was a silence and we both realized we had nothing whatsoever to say to each other. I got up to leave when he took my arm.

'Perhaps you still need a valet?'

I looked down at him. His hair was very thin on top and I noticed a small scar on his cheek.

'I don't think so,' I replied. 'Thanks all the same. Goodbye.'

I hurried out. I don't forget too easily and I wasn't going to return to the miserable relationship we had had before. This man was a thorn in the flesh, and deserved nobody's sympathy. However, I knew he would run after me and so I slowed down.

'You can't run out on me now, sir,' he said. 'You need my help.'

'*Your* help?' I cried, astounded. The cheek of the man. 'Your help? The last thing I want is your help. Don't you ever learn? Go away and pray to your tin God.'

'How do you know he's tin?' he replied quietly.

I looked at him. There was something strange about him. Something compelling. Of course, physically, he didn't look well. I was an Adonis compared to him. But his character somehow had changed. He seemed more assured. More at ease with life. In a way, it was rather relaxing. I shrugged him aside, and walked to the doors of the foyer. As I opened them, the mist swirled in. It

163

would be impossible to go far in this weather, especially as it would soon be dark. How convenient.

'I thought you were going to become a monk,' I said.

There was no answer and I noticed that Catesby had walked across to the chaise-longue, and had sat down. It was the same chaise-longue as before. I sat next to him.

'I thought you were going to become a monk.'

'No,' he answered, 'it's not for me. It would only be an escape.'

'From what?' I asked.

'From her. From you.'

His eyes turned towards me, and their sadness made me look away. I shivered.

'Have you … seen her lately?' I said quietly.

'Of course not,' he replied. 'Of course I haven't. Isn't that an odd question? Considering … '

'I don't know. Tell me. Is it?'

'You need me,' he said again. 'Let me come and work for you.'

I laughed at his effrontery.

'I have a valet. I don't need you.'

'You haven't a valet,' he said. 'You haven't anybody. They've all gone. Haven't they?'

I couldn't bear this any longer, so I stood up and began to walk away.

'You have no right to say that. What have *you* got?' I shouted. 'What exactly have *you* got?'

'Exactly the same as you, of course. Nothing. Except God.'

'Ha!' I threw that at him. 'What drivel. If you have to take God's name, don't do it in vain. God! What has He ever done for you?'

'I don't know,' Catesby replied, walking ahead of me to the door. 'I don't know. But it's nice to know He's there.'

'How *do* you know He's there? Where are the signs? He should have worn his reincarnation in his buttonhole.'

'You said that before. It's becoming a platitude and it doesn't mean a thing. I'll see you in New York.'

'No, you won't. I don't ever want to see you again. You sicken me.'

'In a month. In New York. Goodbye, sir.'

And then he left. He has followed me here just to torment me. That is obvious. He's trying to provoke me.

'By the way, sir.'

I spin round. He has come back and is standing at the door. In his hand there is an orange.

'By the way, sir, why did you change your name to Malmedy?'

'Change it? But that's my name. I never *changed* it to Malmedy. I *am* Malmedy.'

Catesby smiled as if to humour me, and said:

'As you wish, sir. I won't tell a soul. But I can't understand why you had to change it. Especially to Malmedy. It's a very ugly name. What are you running away from?'

'I'm not running away from anything!'

'Except, of course, from Antonella.'

It was then that I hit him. I brought back my fist and hit him, and as he went down I kicked him in the groin. I heard him gasp for breath and I kicked him again in the head. And in the eyes. Each one. Over and over again till the blood spattered over my shoes and on to the floor. He never tried to defend himself, nor shout for help. Perhaps that's why I stopped before it was too late. I stopped and hurried away into the dark air and was soon lost in the mist.

*　　　*　　　*

I am alone. I am utterly alone. On my feet I have slotted empty Kleenex boxes to protect me from the germs on the floor. My hands are encased in polythene bags tied around the wrist by string. I send my suits to be cleaned eight times a day, and never open the windows for fear of pollution. The disease in New York is terrifying. It's in all the papers. I have cut my hair short for fear of bugs and I never go out. I eat almost nothing because all food is contaminated and in my ears I have wadded sealing wax to keep out earwigs. Since I am alone and since I never move, there is nothing for me to hear. I wear only a sheet which I change every four hours since the body sweats whether we know it or not. I spend all my time sitting in the empty bath because it is easier to keep clean, and because I need to shower every half an hour. I have medicated wadding in my mouth around my gums which forces out my face and makes me look almost anthropoid. I don't care. Who is there to see me? I have learnt to defecate only once every two days, and I always breathe through my nose, since the mouth is a great receiver of germs. There is no time in here. I might have been here for weeks. I never move. I just sit with my thoughts and with my eyes closed, since it is impossible not to blink when one's eyes are open, and that naturally attracts dirt. On the wall opposite me, there is nothing. It is just a blank. The bath itself is like a coffin except that I am not dead. I am not alive either. I just am.

*　　　*　　　*

Fifteen days have gone by and I feel much better. I have emerged from my cocoon, and though I am not yet a butterfly, I feel decidedly healthier. I don't go out much. A short walk down to Sixth Avenue to watch the roadworks, and sometimes a stop for a drink at China-town Charlie's. I am stared at and feel self-conscious, but I soon realize that New Yorkers always stare. It is part of their embarrassment.

I then cross to the news-stand at the corner of Fifty-seventh and Sixth, and buy all the magazines with the prettiest covers. *Esquire* and *Vogue* and *House Beautiful* are my favourites because they are nice and shiny and feature beautiful women in absurd clothes which I like. I go back to my room and read these, then I cut out the prettiest photographs and pin them on my wall. I prefer pictures of blondes with wide mouths and have discovered that these are usually English. I have also hired a record player, and yesterday I went to a record shop called The Colony, and asked the man there to choose some records to cheer me up. 'Something to cheer me up,' I said to him. 'Something happy.' He selected six, and I must confess I have never heard of any of the musicians before. Names like Sam Cooke, Mamas and Papas, and Bobby Blue Bland mean nothing to me, but he was a nice man so I took them all, and promised to listen to them carefully. They are in fact rather nice when you hear them for the third time (though not always very happy), and I even find myself singing many of the tunes, especially one that goes:

> All the leaves are brown the leaves are brown
> And the sky is grey the sky is grey-ey.

I can't make out what the third line is, but the fourth has something to do with a winter's day. Yes, I must go and get some more.

The suite, actually, is beginning to look quite nice and homely. It is not the Plaza any more, but it's not too bad. I allow the sun to come in at the windows, and what with the music and the pictures and the flowers I place about the room I feel quite at ease with the world. I even found a print in a book by Arthur Rackham, whom I remember admiring when I was a child. It is an illustration to *The Rhinegold*, and features three nude Rhine maidens surging out of choppy water. They look a bit blue and rather fed up, but what is remarkable is that they are all naked. It makes me wonder whether I noticed that nipple or that bottom as a child, and if I did, what reaction I had. Did it register as much as the rock in the background or the rainbow? Anyway, I know what I feel now and have hung it in the bathroom. You see, I'm getting better and better by the day, and soon I will be able to stand on my own feet without help from the doctors. I am on top of everything.

And then one morning, quite early, I splintered and burnt everything in the sink and crawled back, shivering, into my bath. I sat there, naked, curled up in my bath and shivered with cold, and when Catesby phoned two days later, I cried when he asked if he could come round.

* * *

'The mind of a bigot is like a mole in the earth. The more light you shed upon it, the more it digs deeper into its own darkness.'

'Do you think I'm a bigot?'

'No, but I think you run away from the light. Look at this room. When I found you, you were cowering in the bath. Isn't that an escape?'

'Perhaps it's a fetish. You haven't seen me for nineteen years. You don't know what kinks I have. Perhaps it's a fetish of mine.'

'Drink your milk, sir. It's getting cold.'

168

It was all right with Catesby for a few days. He was a good sort really. Very kind and helpful and he never complained, but he looked as though he'd suffered a lot. He looked after me, looked after my needs. At first I thought he might be queer, and was ready to fire him, but that didn't seem to be the case. Not as far as I could see. We would talk for hours into the night (he slept in an adjoining room, in case you're wondering), and usually the subject was women. Women in general, of course. Not one in particular. He resented my carnal attitude towards the opposite sex, though he respected my philosophy. I, in my turn, quarrelled with his strictly romantic view which I considered had gone out with troubadors and conical hats. He asked me why, and I said that it was the women who had destroyed Romance, and not men. He couldn't understand that, being practically a virgin and a hermit, but I believe it is true. We often played games, like Scrabble or gin rummy and it was almost a week before I realized I hadn't left the room once. Not only that, I had been celibate for five weeks, including the time of my illness, which was, of course, miraculous. But in fact I never felt better in my life, both physically and mentally.

Catesby insisted I ate regularly and even got me to read some books. The only thing I did refuse to tolerate was his continual harping on religion. It embarrassed me, and I knew why. Lately, I had begun to feel guilty. I tell you this quite openly, because it is a key to my character, which sometimes dominates everything I do. In the past year, I had begun to feel guilty for my life. I had begun to doubt. And furthermore, I had begun to think again about God. Now you understand why I resented Catesby. He was hitting below my emotional belt, and it hurt. When he began on the topic, I would always change the subject immediately.

He asked me once while I was cleaning my shoes if I had ever been in love.

'Perhaps,' I replied. 'I like to think so.'

I avoided of course the subject of A.

'I remember the first time I said "*I love you*",' I continued. 'I remember feeling the words ricochetting into every panic corner of my existence.'

'You sound almost human,' Catesby had replied with a smile.

I didn't know how to take that, but his remarks were beginning to irritate me. I knew it was because they were too accurate, but all the same, I was annoyed.

'The stories I'd read about you', he went on, 'always described an insatiable lecher who was utterly selfish and without a care in the world. Malmedy, the great lover. You were always arriving or leaving and at times you reminded me of a robot. You're not a robot are you, sir?'

'I haven't looked lately,' I replied.

'Pardon?'

'It doesn't matter. Besides, your ignorance cramps my conversation.'

And it did. It did. After a fortnight I suddenly realized I had had enough. Why was I tolerating this beggar who had wormed his way into my confidence? I was becoming a vegetable, allowing myself to succumb to his insults. I didn't need him, and in order to prove that to myself I had to get out. I also needed to return to my old life where I was, at least, at ease. I was no longer in darkness and my eyes were open.

One evening about this time Catesby returned to the room as usual with a bag of groceries and some fruit. It had been raining and I noticed he had forgotten his coat. I mentioned this fact and also commented on the unpredictability of New York weather, but he didn't say anything. Then, as he was placing the carton of Borden's milk into the refrigerator, he turned towards me and said:

'Antonella doesn't exist, you know. You must believe that. She really doesn't exist.'

The next day, Catesby was dead.

*   *   *

And so was I.

13

On the morning of the next day, I left my bed early, in order to leave the building before Catesby awoke. I had slept hardly a wink during the night, since my mind was filled with plans and petty conversations. Catesby's words to me had stung me, because I knew them to be lies. He was obviously still jealous of me, and wanted Antonella for himself. I could tell the symptoms. I knew. He wanted me to think that he could sneak in and take her. All the attention he had been giving me in the past fortnight had been a mere blind. A deceit. He was trying to lull me into a state of complacency, so that he could make a move while my back was turned. The fool! As if I couldn't see through it all. Besides, she wouldn't have him. Not her. She wouldn't have this sentimental old dreamer. What did *he* know of women anyway? He had once skirted the perimeter of a girl's perfume, but other than that, nothing. Nothing. I smiled and packed my BOAC holdall and left the room.

It was a nice day outside. Bright and sunny and warm. Men were walking around without jackets, taxi-drivers drove with their left hands on the roofs of the cabs, and women experimented with new dresses. It was spring and I was in a mood for walking. I had never really seen New York, except from the back of a car, and even then it was always the area around Fifth Avenue, and the bright side of Broadway. I hadn't really been around.

I remember I walked for hours, just strolling along the streets gazing into shops, and stopping now and then at a bar. Once I looked up and shaded my eyes and watched a helicopter circle and then descend on to the roof of the Pan Am building, like a fly on to a tall cake. I looked into the faces of girls and into the eyes of old women, and found myself at the river near Queensboro Bridge, and then began to amble back in the direction of the park. I suppose I must have reached the grass in the early afternoon because it was filled with secretaries and clerks, but they soon returned to their offices and I was in the company of children and dogs. Central Park is almost unique. It hasn't the rambling flatness of the London parks, nor the clinical order of the Luxembourg Gardens. Instead, it appears to be a mixture of the prehistoric (elbows of granite emerging out of the soil, dark trees, quick menace) and the picture book. I am not too partial to the quaint little bridges and the ducks, and I think those pretentious little pony-traps are rather hard to take on an empty stomach. They always seem to contain the same red-faced man and the same demi-monde woman, who appear to spend their time avoiding each other's eyes and controlling a primitive urge to wave. But, all in all, it's a pleasant park to stroll in, with one's jacket over one's shoulder and a half-smile on one's mouth.

I took in a quick tour of the zoo (the second lion on the left amuses me), and then decided to find a nice quiet spot to sit down and undo my tie. I would find somewhere shaded and private with no one around. Perhaps in this part of the wood or over there near that bench. Or perhaps, just across there to the left, in that quiet spot near the tall tree where that young girl is sitting. Can you see her? She has blonde hair and is wearing a white dress decorated with blue ribbons.

*   *   *

The detective on my right is called Diamond, and the one in the front of the car is called Tarnowski. I think he's Polish (I wonder if he was in the parade?) and has been quite friendly, but I have ignored him. I am well aware of his methods.

'I could of course sue you for unlawful arrest,' I say without a tremor in my voice. 'I could do that.'

Neither of them say a word. The one next to me is trying to behave casually and is lighting a cigarette. A Camel.

'Did you hear what I said? I realize now why you are against the Civilian Review Board. Oh, it's very clear to me. I'll write to the Mayor and complain. It might be a fun city for him, but it's hell for me.'

They don't listen. I ask if they could open a window since it is very hot, but they don't listen. I wonder where we are going, at this time of the day on a fine day like this.

*   *   *

I am in a room. It is about eight feet by ten feet, and is painted dark green, except for the ceiling and the wood-work which is brown. There is no carpet on the floor and only one window. A sash-cord affair. Two filing cabinets punctuated by cardboard markers and a long photo of a group of men posing outside a large building with pillars. A Coca-Cola calendar and a clipping board and on one wall is a street map of Manhattan, divided into precincts. One of the precincts has more finger marks than the others. Pinned below it, by a drawing pin, is a newspaper photo of Julie Christie's face. She is staring solemnly into the camera, and if one didn't know who she was, one would think she was a murderer's victim or the neighbour's missing child. Since the room is unbearably hot, the air-conditioner is on, though at times the noise is more irritating than the heat. It is wedged through the window, and partially hidden by a plastic Venetian blind. Two slats in the centre of the blind which correspond in height to the eyes of the average man are bent permanently out of place. If one were to look through, one would be able to see Lexington Avenue eight floors below, and sometimes hear the sound of car horns and the intermittent screech of brakes. But generally, this was impossible since we are too high up and the office is usually too busy to hear a thing.

There are two desks in the room. One is against a wall and contains a typewriter and a telephone. Behind it sits a middle-aged police sergeant who is typing with two fingers. He is in uniform but his jacket hangs on the back of his chair, and his shirt collar is undone. He is almost completely bald and looks vaguely Italian in features. He will sit and type throughout the whole scene, and not once will he look up except to work out the spelling of a word, or to dry-run a rather complex sentence. At the other desk, I am sitting. I have been here for about half an hour, and have spoken to no one. Once or twice, the door of the office has opened and Detective Diamond has entered, glanced at me, then left again, but otherwise I have been left alone. I have smoked three cigarettes and have had to use the metal paper-bin as an ashtray. On the desk before me is a telephone, a sheet of blank paper and a pen. That is all. I have just sat and listened to the air-conditioner and the typewriter. Oh, once, Tarnowski entered and offered me some coffee but I refused emphatically. One can never be too careful.

Finally, at about four o'clock, Diamond came back again and closed the door. He was carrying a file of papers which he set down on the desk opposite me, and then pulled up a chair. He had taken his jacket off and I could see the dark circles of sweat on his short-sleeved shirt, and I noticed that once he had placed a leaky ball-point pen in his breast pocket, for the stain was still there. He was about thirty-five years of age, very heavily built but with a paunch. Not a handsome man, but I should think many women would find him attractive. His hair was dark and thick and he had a fine jaw-line and a strong mouth. I must admit, I rather liked the man and suspected that privately he was a good husband who worried a great deal about school fees and the state of the Yankees. I accepted a cigarette from him and waited. He seemed to be in no hurry, for he slowly glanced through the papers in the file, keeping them hidden from me, then left the room. He returned with a plastic ashtray and placed that between us. I noticed another man had entered with him, a Negro, and had sat on a chair in the corner, just out of my line of vision. The typing continued regardless.

'What is your name again?' Diamond asked casually, idly rolling a dead match between forefinger and thumb.

'Do I have to answer these questions?' I replied, unsure of police protocol.

'No,' was the answer. It sounded bored and apathetic, and as if its owner was being more inconvenienced than I. It startled me somehow.

'Malmedy,' I said. 'My name is Malmedy.'

There was a fractional pause and then the piece of blank paper was pushed in front of me, and the pen placed in my hand. I wrote down MALMEDY and underlined it. Diamond twisted the paper towards him and grunted, then held it up so that the Negro could see it. It was then placed on the desk before the detective who began to doodle on it. Straight lines and curlicues. Nothing too profound.

'You live in Manhattan?' Diamond asked.

'At the moment, yes. I have ... a room. East Eighty-eighth Street. Number four hundred and three.'

I noticed that the Negro was writing all this down.

'Married?'

'No. You would know that if you read the papers.'

'Why would I know that?'

'Well ... didn't you see the interview with me? It was in a magazine. Didn't you see it? It was rather fun.'

'Let's hope this one will be a lot of laughs too.'

Diamond then walked towards the window and looked out. I stubbed out my cigarette.

'Did you know that the murder rate in New York is almost the highest in the world?'

'No, I didn't but I'll take your word for it,' I said.

'The statistics aren't very pretty.'

'They never are.'

'I work hard. Twelve, fifteen hours a day sometimes. Pay is pitiful. My wife moans at me because I'm never home. I have a son I haven't seen for ten days but he lives in the same house. I am not liked by strangers and my neighbours ignore me. I have a scar on my back as long as a pencil, and I possess only one suit. Last week, I found I had piles. Why then do you think a man like me sticks a job like this?'

'Loyalty,' I said. 'A desire to uphold justice and fight crime.'

'Are you trying to be funny?'

'No,' I said quickly, and then added with polite curiosity:

'Why do you?'

'What?'

'Stick a job like this?'

'I'm a sado-masochist.'

I laughed. So did Diamond. He had a fine sense of humour, I thought. But he looked very tired. Perhaps he'd just come off night shift. He walked back to the desk and sat down.

'It was very nice of you to come here,' he said quietly.

'Anything I can do, just ask. I'm not a man to shy away from—'

'We could tell that. We took one look and we could tell that. Didn't we, Harry?'

Harry grinned.

'A lot of interesting things happen in this precinct.'

'I'm sure they do,' I commented.

'Every day, a new adventure.'

'I can well believe it.'

'A new slice of life.'

'On your doorstep.'

'On our doorstep. Take this morning. It's a nice day. Sunny. You probably noticed, being a man of perception.'

'Yes, I did,' I replied. 'In fact, I took advantage of it and went for a walk.'

'Exercise does you good. Tarnowski and I went for walk too. To the park. We often do that. We drive down to Fifty-ninth Street and take a walk. It starts the day. Do you know what we saw? This morning?'

'A squirrel?'

'Well, we saw plenty of those. Something else though? Guess.'

'A ... an elephant?'

'Now you're teasing us. Be serious. What do you think we saw?'

I smiled and tried to join in the spirit of the game.

'People going to work. Using the park as a short cut.'

'Warm. Very warm. Anything else, you think?'

'I'm not much good at games.'

'Try. You're doing very well.'

'Well ... I'm sure you must have seen at least one pretty girl.'

'Very good. That's exactly what we saw. Harry? He guessed it in three.'

Harry gave me a round of applause. I bowed.

'What do you think the pretty girl looked like?' Diamond asked, lighting another cigarette.

'Oh, I don't know that,' I replied. 'Like her?' I pointed at the newspaper photo on the wall.

'Same colour hair. But different face.'

'It's very hard to describe a pretty girl. It's a matter of taste.'

'Of course it is. I go for the big busty girls like Sophia Loren. Harry here, though, thinks she's a monstrosity and prefers skinny girls. Like *her*. As you say, it's a matter of taste. Tell me, what kind of girl do you prefer?'

'Well,' I said, leaning back in the chair, 'if she is blonde, then I would add deep-blue eyes and a wide mouth. Soft features and ... well, young perhaps. About sixteen. Though, don't think I'm a paedophiliac. I'm just giving you one type that happens to come to mind.'

'Uncanny. You're uncanny. I admire you. Do you go in for quiz shows at all? You'd make a fortune.'

'Thank you,' I said humbly.

'It's a pleasure. The girl we saw was just like you described. To the letter.'

My eyes widened.

'What was she doing?' I asked.

'She wasn't doing anything. She was dead. I told you we had an interesting life.'

'Yes ... '

I looked away. The three men in the room seemed to be very cool about the whole affair.

'That's very tragic,' I said. 'Finding a young girl like that.'

'Isn't it?' Diamond said. 'Isn't it just? She had been beaten to death only a few yards from the road.'

I nodded sympathetically.

'It's one of those days. Often happens in the hot weather. You can understand how I feel, being a father as well.'

'I do,' I said. 'I do indeed. I hope you catch the murderer.'

'Well, we do too. Which is why we're so pleased you offered to help us.'

'I didn't know it was for … that. I mean, how could I help?'

'Well, we don't know yet. By the way, take your jacket off if you like. It's very stifling in here.'

'I'm all right. I … prefer it on.'

'Well, if you change your mind.'

I smiled and got up to stretch my legs. The police sergeant continued typing, oblivious.

'Your name's Catesby, isn't it?' Diamond said suddenly.

'Pardon?' I replied, spinning round towards him.

'I said your name is Catesby. Isn't that right?'

I laughed.

'No, that's not my name. My name's Malmedy. Catesby's not *my* name.'

Diamond frowned and studied the papers on the desk. 'Isn't it?'

'No,' I said with a smile. 'It's Malmedy. Remember, you asked me right at the beginning. I even wrote it down. Fancy thinking *I'm* Catesby.'

'Oh yes. Of course. I know why I said Catesby. I was looking at the wrong page. No, Catesby is the man we're looking for.'

'Looking for?'

'Yes. He's our suspect. For the murder of the girl.'

I stared at him, wide-eyed. Catesby? A murderer? I couldn't believe it. It must be another—

'How—how do you know?'

'Well, we're not sure, of course, but several witnesses saw a man answering to his description running away and one of them, a Mrs Friedberg, recognized him as being a tenant in her rooming house.

'Mrs Friedberg?'

'Yes. She has a rooming house in East Eighty-eighth Street.'

'I know,' I said. 'I live there too.'

'Well, that's why we thought you could help us. We wondered if you knew this man, Catesby. Harry went round to the place, but the suspect wasn't there. Any idea where he might be? We gather you knew him well.'

I was about to answer, when Tarnowski entered. In his hand was a photograph. He took a look at me to see if I was still there, and then showed the photo to Diamond. The two men exchanged a few words in a low breath, then Tarnowski left the room and closed the door again. I became aware that the police sergeant had stopped typing. He had stopped typing and was looking at me. I turned away. Harry, the Negro, blew his nose.

'This is interesting,' said Diamond finally.

'What is?' I asked.

'I wasn't talking to you.'

'I'm sorry,' I said quickly.

'That's all right. I didn't mean to shout. I was going to tell Harry that this photograph is interesting. It's of the dead girl. It looks as though it was taken fairly recently.'

He held the picture up so that I could see. It wasn't a very good photograph and was rather over-exposed. It showed a girl standing in a field, and posing rather gauchely for the camera. There was nothing very remarkable about it, and I assumed that Diamond had found it interesting because the girl was obviously pregnant.

'See that? It looks as though she's pregnant,' he said.

'Yes, I noticed that. It certainly looks that way.'

'You don't recognize her at all?' Diamond said. 'You don't by any chance know who she is?'

'Oh yes,' I said, looking closely at the picture. 'Oh yes. Her name, I believe, is Antonella.'

* * *

They dropped me off at the rooming house at six o'clock the same evening. I told them I was sure Catesby would come back to the place, especially if I were there, for I was the only friend he had. Diamond thought it was a good idea, and said they would wait till I called. They were very understanding.

It is impossible for me to describe how grief-stricken I was when I realized that Antonella was no longer alive. I had to have medical attention. It was a great blow. And yet, oddly, I was in a way faintly relieved, as if a great burden had been taken off my back. Perhaps you understand that. Perhaps you have understood that all along. Ever since the beginning. But I didn't. Not at first. In a way, it was inevitable. Antonella was dead. *Is* dead. She had been murdered by Catesby of all people. I am too confused to understand why. What *are* the motivations that guide some people? So often there is no rational explanation. It is understandable, when one realizes that the greatest motivations in the world are irrational, if treated scientifically.

I close the door of the room, but refrain from switching

on the light. Then, crossing to the window, I quickly detach the draw-strings from the curtains and knot them together. I have long since decided my plan of action. It is between Catesby and I, for we are one. I cannot avoid the reality of my mind any more, which is sad, because lately I have for the first time in years touched my own sanity. I fashion the cord into a noose, and wait. Only I can be his executioner. Only I can be that.

When he finally arrives, creeping up the back stairs like a spider, I seize him immediately. He doesn't struggle. I think he *wants* me to end it all. I tie one end of the cord to the banister rail (we are on the fourth floor) and slip the noose around his neck. I avoid his eyes as they stare at me, and before he can pray to his God, I push him over the rail into the void of the well. He drops, falls, spins down and then the rope tightens. I feel it choking me, cutting into my flesh, and my eyes begin to bulge and I feel my bowels opening. For a brief second in time, I see the flights of stairs spinning round me as my feet struggle for a footing, but there is nothing. The cord strains and jerks back and my neck is broken. There is no blinding re-run of my life, no hallucinations, no repentance. There is just light, and I, Catesby, am blissfully dead at last. My nightmare is over.

Part Three

TRANSITION

OBITUARY

THOMAS
EDWARD
CATESBY

Thomas Edward Catesby, 38, the
English playboy and millionaire,
died by his own hand in New York
yesterday. A celebrated eccentric and
self-styled Don Juan of the post-war
years, he became notorious in 1957
when he was found guilty of the
murder of his fiancée, Antonella
Nuages in Brioge, France. Following
a plea of insanity, he was put under
psychiatric care, but his schizophrenia was complicated by a severe
guilt complex and total withdrawal,
and in 1958 he was taken to Rosewell
Institute in New York where he was
to remain until his death. He never
recovered from his illness, despite the
use of drugs and other methods,
though in recent months he had
shown an encouraging improvement;
the true cause of his disease was
never accurately established.

AFTERWORD

And so I am still here. Not a sound. Not a word, you whisper to me. I strain my eyes in the darkness and hear nothing. Are you angry because I deceived you? Please don't be. It is myself I deceived. No one else. If only I had been strong before that moment when the cord straightened. But it was tragic. Oh, it was tragic. I tried. I …

And now I am in this box, under this earth, left only with my own thoughts. This is hell. I have found it. This is hell and I am in it. I lie for ever, for eternity, accompanied only by thoughts of my wretched life and visions of her. They cannot drive me mad for I am mad. And sane too. I am everything and I am nothing. I am that grub I talk so much about. I am the receptacle for my own torment. Each memory impales me like an arrow and I scream. But who can hear? You? No. Oh, no. No one. Oh God, I am in your hell, aren't I? I am here in it. Isn't that what you wanted? Oh, if only you didn't exist. Then I wouldn't either and I would be at peace. Peace … Instead I am just alone. As in life, I am in death. My mind is my coffin and it can never decay. Lean closer to me and let me whisper in your ear. Let me speak. *My father died when I was eight years old. He was buried ten years later when his heart finally stopped beating.* I begin again. *It was a merciful moment of departure for him and a bitter one for me.* This hell in me begins again. And again. *And that, really, is all that can be said about him, and all that I would ever want to say, without malice and without sadness, for that was the relationship we had.*

And again …